Cover art: Stephanie Murdoch

Paul and Floral

ISBN	978-0-473-67083-2	Epub
ISBN	978-0-473-67084-9	Kindle
ISBN	978-0-473-67085-6	PDF
ISBN	978-0-473-67085-3	Print

Omine Secundo (Under Favourable Omen)

The Murdoch Motto.

Paul and Floral

Brett Murdoch

1

A noise infiltrated my agitated mind. A carryover from my dreams?

No. It was a real sound.

A distinct sound, repetitive and harsh. It was clear and close, coming from the corridor. It grew louder until it seemed it was in the room with me.

I recognised it. The squeak from the wheels of the Dead Trolley.

The Dead Trolley – an old gurney with a hooded cover. Although rarely seen, the trolley was often used. This was the vehicle in which most residents of this old people's home would eventually ride.

My fear escalated to panic. They were coming for me. Those in power definitely wanted rid of me. I had been expecting the trolley; I wanted to run but was helpless, unable to resist. I had no strength left. I was easy prey and if I disappeared, who would know or care?

The squeaking stopped. The trolley was outside my door.

They're coming in. They can't do this.

Maybe it would be painless. *What do they do? A huge surge of morphine?*

No further movement in the corridor – silence all around, apart from my laboured panting.

I trembled. Fear held me tight. My heart pounded; each beat a surge of blood roaring in my ears.

Moments passed. Minutes? Half an hour? It seemed an eternity.

Then the squeak recommenced and began to diminish. The trolley was moving away. The sound died out. They had gone.

This time, they had gone.

I was sitting bolt upright in my bed. I flopped back into my pillows, exhausted, my nerves a-jangle. Was this their warning? A reminder of their power over me, of life and death? Was it a harbinger of my forthcoming fate?

I was now even more certain that I was neither keen, nor ready to leave this world, and certainly not like that. Whatever happened I must conquer my fear, my helplessness. I cursed my situation, which was largely caused by my uncooperative belligerence, my rudeness, my ignorance of my status. As well as by the badness here.

It was 6.30am. I had been awake for hours. The gloom of my spartan room, dimly lit in green by the digital clock, was lightening slightly in the dawn.

Grey light through grey curtains: a reflection of my life.

How had it all come to this?

Claire, my wife, had deserted me some fifteen years ago. I blamed her still. She had gone into The Halsey Road Clinic, a private surgical hospital here in Auckland, for a relatively common, straightforward procedure to correct her intermittently accelerated heartbeat. All had gone well; we were pleased. We chatted happily in the hospital room after the operation. I went home that evening and arranged to collect her the following day.

This was not to be.

I was phoned in the middle of the night. My wife had gone into cardiac arrest and had died. They had tried hard, but couldn't save her.

I was broadsided.

I had been ten years older than Claire, and had never imagined I'd outlive her. She had been fit and young for her age. She was lovely. She brimmed with kindness; an empathetic soul who carried an aura of gentle sadness about her. Claire had been my interface with the world, the foil to my social ineptitude. It was she who wrote the notes of gratitude and support, sent the cheering flowers, and made the phone calls to stay close to family and friends.

My life had changed, then. Her slim, soft body, her fine auburn hair, the deep, warm looks … gone.

The house progressively became my entire world. An elderly man rattling around in a big old colonial villa.

I had never been particularly gregarious, and found it difficult to keep up contact with friends and acquaintances. Indeed, they seemed to have changed; suddenly they seemed vacuous and boorish.

2

I awoke agitated and confused. I'd been moved from my usual room. I didn't know it then, but the move was from the Cheshire Block (standard care) to the Priestly Block (high care secure).

These were residential sections within the Winston Churchill Retirement Village. On the night I heard the Dead Trolley, I had been there for three years.

Why and how I had been moved would remain a mystery to me. I certainly didn't recall being consulted about it. I'd gone to bed, having taken the medication given to me, in 'Independent with Aid', only to awake in 'High Care Secure'.

By then I was fast losing my connection with life, even my connection with the daily here and now. For better or for worse, at least I was aware of this decline.

The gentle voice of carer Floral Ramos pushed through the fog: "They are doing this to you Paul because you causing them very much trouble. The main boss Dhama is very angry."

"But …" I feebly protested, before rallying a bit, "calling that evilness a 'moronic assemblage of surgical discards' hardly warrants attempted murder."

"You be joking again," Floral said quietly. "Not funny to these men. They can do bad things to you. You listen to me careful now. You must be no trouble at all."

"What do I care anyway?" I replied. "What does it matter, as old as I am, and now virtually immobile. Let the creeps kill me. I just don't care."

I had disliked Dhama from the time I first arrived. He was Indian or Sri Lankan, in his early fifties. He always dressed in a charcoal-grey suit which suffered from iron-sheen and was a size too big. His black hair was oiled down – stuck slick to his pate. He was a charmless man who carried with him a permanent air of disdain.

We were interrupted by sounds in the corridor outside my door. Floral's face tightened; she quickly moved away from my bedside, and then, from across the room, started to chastise me for being uncooperative. She interrupted her rant to hold a finger to her lips.

The door pushed open and Dhama and his small group of staff – sycophants each and every one – strode in.

The staff were mimicking Dhama's aggressive pose: chins thrust forward, mouths down in distaste. An unsavoury interaction for them, no doubt. They strode forward as one and loomed over my bed.

"Ah …" I suppressed an insult. "Ah, chief manager, sir," I croaked.

Floral stood with her back to me, fussing in an affected way at the bedside table. She nodded slightly at my constraint.

"Moodys," began Dhama, "your Enduring Power of Attorney and the home geriatrician are fully of agreement that for you protection, and protections of all things, and for other residents also, you confined to High Care Secure future forwards. Mr Varahuchuse being most good man and full owner of Winston Churchill Village, and being much generous fellow, is allowing television you room, but not for you be attending happy hour, or of having the conservatory time. Indeed, this now the case is.

"Carer Ramos –" he turned to Floral and continued, "we not be paying very much the OT so you need finish your shift now, being is past the eight a.m."

"Yes, Mr Dhama, soon be going," said Floral coquettishly.

The visit was concluded. They had delivered their message. Dhama's rotund, sloppily besuited form turned, and he and the belligerent ones left.

The usually locked door hung provocatively unclosed in their wake.

"I must to be going. I come and see you early tomorrow. I have the full access this wing now. Silly you, Paul! You must be good now, please!" Floral chided me, frowning with concern as she did so.

"Yes, pretty flower," I replied. "Thank you."

Floral filled my water tumbler for me and left, locking the door behind her.

My mind returned to the past. I had been beyond official retirement age when my wife died, and although I continued a few directorships and did some management consulting work, eventually the ineptitude of the semi-corporate organisations I worked for became tiresome and my consequent cynicism more and more difficult to suppress.

Eventually I gave up all work.

In earlier times I had my own business, a boutique-scale export consultancy and business advisory practice. We specialised in supporting small-to-medium enterprises that were struggling, particularly with their export markets. Additionally we filled in for local body organisations that needed short-term support. We had done well. We had made good money. After a good offer, I sold the business to a Singapore-based, Chinese-owned business consultancy called Red Star.

My life drifted on. My life contracted.

My dreams that night were vivid. They were technicolour and sharply focused. As is usually the case, to me they were not dreams. They were big screen reality. I had become a younger version of myself – not as I had really been when younger, but a stronger, wiser, more successful version of me.

Floral accompanied me in my dreams, but now she was Florence. Florence was like Floral but a young version with striking good looks. She was physically transformed, now a superwoman – lithe, strong and fearless. Together we undertook several crusades in which we found and avenged the victims of evildoing. We dispensed harsh justice summarily on the perpetrators of the wrongs. We acted with clinical efficiency and zealous righteousness.

While still lashing out in the brutal close fighting around me I was yanked back, wide awake, into the dark, small hours of my little room. I lay in my bed jittery, sweating heavily, my old heart thumping in my chest.

Along with the returning awareness of where I was physically, the awareness of my life situation returned. I was afraid. My fear turned my sweat to a cold chill. I lay there desperately trying to regain some composure.

Floral would be here soon. Perhaps she could help me. Could someone from the outside world be contacted? Surely something could be done. How did I become this prison inmate? An irritating old man – yes, but why did they want me gone? Was it like this for others here? That was an awful thought. Perhaps my cynicism and belligerence were intolerably provocative. Perhaps they had space and cost/benefit considerations, and I was financially unviable.

Most of the other vulnerable residents were probably benign and easy, and consequently were made comfortable and were contented. I imagined too, that their loved ones would afford them protection by their presence, concern, and vigilance.

I had no control of my life – no means of communication and no resources to use. I had no doting loved ones to care for me.

Undoubtedly the Home had access to my money via my unchosen life representative – my Enduring Power of Attorney. This EPA was an automaton named Gerald Tranche who had been selected for me. I had met him just once.

Furthermore, the home probably had an arrangement with my benign but cold-hearted and greedy lawyer, Rowena Gillespie, with whom I now had no contact and no means of contacting.

Had I been classified as a totally dependent dementia patient?

When I had arrived here, the doctor had deemed it necessary I should have a plaster cast on my leg to support the fracture in my femur. This simple procedure had been very painful, and they had sedated me with one of those preoperative tranquilizers.
Something had gone wrong, and consequently I lost ten of my remaining days.

I had passed out completely and was apparently in La La Land for those days. Unable to communicate, and with no family or friends to advocate for me, I had been appointed an EPA by the state. Tranche was just as I would have imagined a freelance EPA to be: overweight, poor personal hygiene, a comb-over, and smeary horn-rimmed glasses.

Gillespie, my lawyer, was a good-looking, youngish woman. She was tall with honey blonde hair and unusual blue-green eyes. She had taken the business over when my old friend and lawyer, Frank Holly, retired. I would discover, however, that Rowena Gillespie, for all her charming ways, had a cold, venal heart.

I needed to think – to concentrate.

Yes, resurrect your woozy brain and keep it clear.

Think.

My priority was to avoid the morphine-pump exit that seemed preordained. How to evade this terminal stop and its gruesome realities? I was exhausted by these troubled thoughts after my fear-filled night.

Even though it was light, I fell into an unsettled sleep.

Claire and I had one child together. A boy, Johnny. Sadly, Johnny was unlike either of us.

Johnny was the disappointment of my life.

When he reached his early twenties he moved away to the Philippines. We rarely heard from him after that, although I suspect he used to contact his mother to ask her for money. Johnny was the one thing that Claire and I did not, could not, discuss. She found it impossible to face up to the type of person our son really was, whereas I had reconciled to the fact that our son was a nasty human being. I wished to know nothing of his dodgy dealings and life of sleaze.

The boy had been well brought up. We had given him love and every care. His mother had doted on him. We had tried, and tried, all the more so, as things progressively unravelled. The effort we put in made the situation all the harder to bear. He had been sent to good schools and had been given every opportunity.

Johnny was also physically unlike either of us. He was thickset with a square, shapeless, body. He had a squarish head too, and wiry sandy hair. Claire and I were both slender with dark hair and, I thought, with some look of elegance.

From the start the boy had been devious and calculating. Throughout his childhood, particularly as he got older, we had been summoned to his school, Saint Kentigern's, for 'a chat', either about his lack of progress, or his latest episode of outrageous behaviour. This often involved bullying, and sometimes dishonesty. Discipline was a joke to Johnny – literally a joke.

We were at our wits' ends for years. We cried together.

When Johnny left to go overseas, it was a huge relief for me. I don't think the pain ever subsided for Claire.

"Are you only sleeping or being dead already?" Floral's concerned but teasing voice eased me back into the world. She had quietly unlocked the door and was beside my bed. I mentally hauled myself up.

"I'm doing for you a good breakfast and proper tea with the pot that you like," she said, smiling.

"Angels exist," I said, with some effort. I was relieved to have my only, newish, unproven, and unlikely friend back with me.

"Flower," I said, rubbing my forehead. "Bad things have been happening and my goodness, I must get out of here. I'm very afraid. I'm sure they are deliberately frightening me. I think they want to kill me. It sounds fantastical I know, but I am a nuisance to them, and they really dislike me."

I looked Floral in the eye and continued, "Last night they tried to frighten me half to death, and before, when I was moved to this room, I was very heavily drugged."

Floral handed me a tumbler of water which I sipped.

"I know it seems crazy and paranoid, but now that I'm so isolated, I feel I'm at the end of some continuum – one for which there is but one outcome. For them, the sooner the better, I think." I hung my head in dejection.

Floral looked at me with kindness and concern. "Much bad place here, Paul," she said. "I try to get you back to rest home section. Then it is hard for them do bad things to you. I will try and do this if you want. In this part of Winston

Churchill, no one can see what goes on, and there are plenty bad people work here."

Floral leaned over and rubbed my shoulder; she tilted her head towards me then helped me sit up.

I needed her help; I just had no energy left. And I needed her help for much more than sitting up.

"Could I get strong enough to walk properly again, do you think?" I asked her. "Can you get me a walking frame so that I can exercise and get stronger?" I could hear the desperation in my voice.

"Many die in the High Care for sure, Paul. Maybe I get you an old walker, but you are not strong to be doing much. They will not let you do the exercises – these men. Many bad people this place – the boss one, and others too. I can help you, Paul. I want to do this for you. I'm pretty clever, not only bad English speaking. These men here bad ones for sure, but they dumb melons also."

"Dumb melons!" I exclaimed. "I'm certainly with you on that. OK then, clever one, let's get me out of this place while I still have a slim chance. But Floral, I am being totally self-absorbed – how are things with you? You seem rather worn out, are they working you too hard, you poor thing?"

"Place I come from in Philippines is Mindanao Island, Paul. From the city of Cagayan de Oro. Hard work always there, especially in old days, and sometime you only work to get rice. Poor person in Philippines need have rice or will die. Not so big of choices in your life unless you very rich person. Want go the doctor, dentist, much money costs. Manga good food and things for the rich person only. Much hard work, or you need to be dodgy. Me, Floral; I working the extra shift here – Winston Churchill and are very pleased to be doing this. Now always I have good food, clothes, and a nice house for me renting. Sometimes I am tired. Yes, but this is only a small trouble for Floral. Everyone have a little trouble, Paul."

"I want to know of your troubles, sweetness," I responded. "I have become obsessed with my own petty problems, and with my insular life. I have lost any semblance of empathy or care for those around me. I am sorry, Floral."

"Not to be sorry Paul, please. My job being to look after you. I am plenty strong too. When having no money the eyes not always see somethings, Paul. My husband get us to the New Zealand using dodgy money from the bad bar he run in Cagayan for the tourist. He get anything for the tourist and for his bad friends. He also get the false documents for the immigration officials here. He get these by giving the bribe of the Philippines official. Oh yes! Philippine is not like the New Zealand. Here is very proper.

"This husband mine, he bringing his bad ways here too. Always has bad ways. He is a man of bad heart. He never changing, I know this."

"Floral, I feel sad for you. You must have had awful times, you poor soul. You deserve a better future. I wish I was able to help," I answered.

"Problems small for Floral. Always plenty full belly and have some good friend, like Angel." Floral gave me a kind smile.

Floral had duties to attend to, and she left.

This chat had given me a glimmer of hope for myself, but I felt much concern for my gentle friend.

Later she returned and we set about formulating a plan. She knew she could not spend too much time with me, or suspicion would be aroused amongst the many 'connected ones' within the staff. She knew I had no means of communication, no mobile phone. She said she could get one for me and that we could hide it somewhere – perhaps in my mattress.

I feared they would find any phone and it would be confiscated, and that this would cause trouble for her. A phone would certainly be some defence, though – even if was only a means to call Floral.

I suggested we used notes for communication with the outside world. With these I could elicit help. Floral could bring them to me and deliver them too. She tried to be positive about this scenario but was a little dismissive too. She thought that notes could be found, and this would worsen things.

Floral said she would ask for fulltime placement on the Secure Wing, and to be my designated primary carer.

As it transpired, our complex communication plans weren't needed.

I had become concerned for Floral; I asked again about her current circumstances. She didn't address these, but was keen to tell me more about her earlier life. Her father had been a shift worker in a pineapple juice processing factory on the outskirts of their town. He was an uneducated man with a love for movies and television stories, and for singing karaoke. He also had a weakness for drugs, which were prevalent and cheap.

Her mother had been a cleaner and had spent much of each night cleaning jeepneys and mini vans. This work brought her little reward.

Her mother died when Floral was thirteen. As Floral described it, her mother had always been lean and delicate, but had died unexpectedly, her lifeless form at rest in an open coffin surrounded with colourful tropical flowers and flickering candles. The cause of death hadn't been ascertained, but Floral thought it was from tuberculosis.

Things had changed profoundly for Floral then, but she was neither shocked nor distraught at her mother's death. She had been very sad, but was pleased that her mother had been released from the pain and drudgery of her joyless life.

She had gained some comfort seeing her mother looking relaxed and peaceful for the first time.

That night my dreams were supercharged. Again, we embarked on our vigilante duties: I was younger and stronger than before, and agile – much like a martial arts hero. I knocked down our assailants like ninepins. I leapt and pirouetted with powerful physicality.

Florence was there beside me, kicking and lunging with deadly effect. This time, although vivid, my dreams did not wake me. I slept through the night and, thankfully, there were no external incidents to terrorise me.

I awoke refreshed, calm, and strong.

Perhaps I had a future after all. Maybe some quality of life could be restored to me for the duration.

3

Along with the morning, and my composure, came a clearer consciousness. I was recharged, felt younger. Perhaps in response to my active dreams I swung my legs over the bed, and I stood for the first time in a long while. I swayed but I stood. "I'm not dead yet," I said to myself. I shuffled forward a step, involuntarily reversed a step back, and then sat unceremoniously down on the bed.

A carer arrived. It was the man who dressed like a woman: Boona. She had blunt features and a dreadful complexion; her eyes were bloodshot and wild. She was always angry. She roughly toileted me, gave me a crude shave, and a slap across the face for good measure – this after I had said, 'Easy-on, pretty lady.' A foolish provocation and stupid of me – or perhaps not. Maybe I shouldn't change too dramatically if we were to succeed: I should remain the cynic, the watcher, the insightful commentator.

Mid-morning, Floral called in. I knew it was her by the gentle unlocking of the door.

"Paul Moody," she began unusually, putting her finger to her lips. "You will be cooperating good for sure after we make you wake up your ideas." Behind her in the hall a shadow fell across the doorway.

That scum; Dhama, no doubt.

"You good behaviour having maybe we give you lounge privilege soon." Floral was looking at me as she spoke, not with a cheery look, but with warning in her eyes.

"Now that would be fabulous," I cautiously replied. "That would be a real treat, company, the television." I suppressed the urge to add: the babble, the smell of urine, the inane television programmes.

Floral fussed with the bed and continued small talk about village goings-on. The shadow in the doorway melted away. Floral hummed a tune and fussed with the bedclothes a little longer. She went to the door and looked out into the corridor.

"Is gone," she said.

"Was that the honourable Dhama?"

"He is very bad for you, Paul. He wants more beds and he very angry that you call him bad names," Floral replied.

"Yes, I've been a little indiscreet; foolish, probably. I've let my ego get the better of my vulnerability. I see that now: cavalier of me, and very stupid. Now, Petal, to work. Can you get a message to my lawyer, do you think? Escape may well be the plan, but I think we should try to get outside help first."

I sat up to drink the tea Floral had bought me. I felt stronger than I had done.

"I check already this for you; your lawyer signing off that Secure Confinement Agreement. That lady not so good, I think," Floral advised.

My mouth dropped, and I blurted, "Signed … a – Secure – Confinement – Agreement! Christ! Do I have access to any help at all? To any money? Can I contact anyone?" I was flustered, my questions rhetorical. "I could write a letter … you – you could take it to someone who will help me. Now, um … who can I write to? Who can I trust?" My mind was blank.

I'd become dysfunctional, defeated, helpless. I had been written off, abandoned by my supposed supporters. I leaned back into the pillows, stressed and unable to think.

"Must be going now, coming back afternoon," Floral said, and she left. She had spent too much time with me as it was. The door lock clicked behind her.

I forced myself to think. My small family were but remnants now. My two best friends – my wife and my brother – long gone. My only remaining relatives were distant ones, and we had long since lost touch. My estranged son was a self-centred bogan with no heart.

Could I go to Social Services, to a church, to any do-gooder outfit? What would I say to them? I had no access to my money. Where was it? Did any remain? It had probably been embezzled by the lawyer and my dodgy EPOA, or even perhaps by this malevolent outfit here.

I had no means of communication, even if I had someone trustworthy to contact.

I spent the next few hours going over scenarios whereby I might get help. How could I get away from here to somewhere safe? How could I recover my money? How could I get some control of my life back?

Everything was too difficult. My circumstances were murky and seemed steeped in corruption. My life had no focal point. No certainty – all those things I had previously taken for granted.

The more I thought about what to do, the more escape seemed the only solution. But with nowhere to go, no money or plan, and with my infirmity, it seemed impossible.

Physically I could barely stand up and shuffle along. I needed help to get to the toilet (although I had been feeling a little stronger and had become a little more mobile over the last few days).

Desperation and helplessness overwhelmed me.

Later Floral returned, as she had promised. I was dozing, as I often did. I did not miss having a television to watch. A radio would have been a welcome distraction though, particularly for the pleasure that music would bring. I did miss music.

The Winston Churchill home is situated on a tidal estuary. Floral took me outside in a wheelchair. The tide was in, and the upper Waitemata Harbour sparkled in the clear light. As the sea birds wheeled in unconstrained freedom above us, they cried out in glee. A songbird sang close at hand.

"Thank you, Floral, this is lovely," I said.

She smiled, and sat on a wooden seat beside me. "Paul, my cousin is giving for you this pill to take." She put two grey capsules in my hand and offered a bottle of water with which to wash them down.

"What are these? I'm feeling OK-ish at the moment," I replied, suspicious of any new medication.

"This is very special for health," she countered. "This one will make you strong like a young man. Trust me on this." Then she swept an arm wide, suggesting an omnipresent wisdom which should always be accepted.

I raised my eyebrows. "An elixir of life perhaps? Fabulous!"

"This not for joking about. This is a special mixture of herbal things for fixing of the ageing and generally for being healthy. Best science is," Floral said, then she continued, "This one fix right into body cells. My cousin clever and working in bio science. Trust of me Pauls. Is working good for me. I feeling much more fit already. You need to be taking this. I will bring it to you each day.

Also, another thing, Paul Moody. I tell you this – I am thinking of coming running away with you. Yes. Like you, Paul, I want to be running away. I am certain about this. I have been thinking much about this." Floral was looking at me intently.

"My goodness," I said. "Not really, my petal? You're just a bit worn out, I expect. Most understandable it is too, having to work in this dungeon with deranged old fellows like me everywhere."

"My life, Paul Moody," she continued, "no bloody good. My husband fat-lazy, no interest Floral, and all time is gambling and does other bad things. No life I have, Paul. I think we should get some money and together go escaping."

"Bravo, Floral. What a wonderful thought; a companion in arms. Better lives for us both. But you must think more about this, my dear; an escape from your present life is a not a straightforward matter I think."

I swallowed the tablets. We went in.

"Needing toilet or anything?" Floral asked when she was about to leave.

I shook my head.

"I mean this, Paul. You think about it. We can do this thing together. You think about planning things. In the morning I come back and we can talk about."

Floral gave me a cheeky, challenging smile, then went off about her duties.

After Claire's death, my life had just meandered along.

I was alone, and empty.

My brother and only sibling, Hamish, had died many years before, and my friends, many of whom were only business colleagues, drifted away or died. Things started to come undone when I found walking exceedingly difficult. 'Mobility issues' the social services folk labelled it. Driving a car had been out of the question for some time by then, and progressively I couldn't get around at all.

I became dependent on outside agencies for everything.

Dr Jacobson, our long-term GP, retired. His replacement, Dr Margaret E'Claire, was very nice and went to every trouble to arrange all manner of support for me.

I stood clinging to a rail under the shower as a stranger washed me.

I hated it.

My innate cynicism, belligerence and pride came into full flower. I struggled to look after myself. Eventually, inevitably, I fell heavily and hurt myself badly. A fractured femur and two broken ribs. A St John ambulance driver and his helper carted me out of the house on a stretcher, over which they draped a light cover to protect me from the drizzle of the cold winter's day.

"You can take that cover off my face. I'm not dead yet," I had berated them.

The bleakest milestone in my life.

My destination on this likely one-way trip: the Winston Churchill Retirement Village. The facility was one of several in a chain that specialised in mid-market old folks' homes. I had been accepted, at a premium fee, as an urgent referral.

The day progressed, the afternoon shift came on and my meal arrived, shepherd's pie with two slices of buttered bread and a punnet of Turkish delight ice-cream. I enjoyed it.

Turkey, as prompted by the ice-cream flavour, reached out to me. Istanbul: bustling Istanbul. Big, old, bustling Istanbul. That would be a great bolthole, if we could only find a way to get there. We would be hard to trace, and it would be hard to extricate us from Turkey too.

Many years earlier, I had assisted in a government-sponsored development project involving the export of milk powder to Turkey and the import of dried fruits and spices from Turkey to New Zealand. Throughout the period when the trade was being established, I had been to Istanbul a number of times and had become enamoured with the city. I had found it more than exotic and fascinating; it had a surreal, magical way about it, and a romance too. I had found it intoxicating.

After my simple but pleasing dinner I lay, trance-like, on my bed. Perhaps due to the surprise and excitement of the events of the day, or, as I began to think, because of something they'd put in my food, I felt outside of my body, and the more I tried to concentrate on plans for the escape, the more my mind drifted into dreams.

Memories swirled around me, and childhood returned.

I was standing on the bare old floorboards of my uncle's beach cottage, in the old Waihi Beach township. It would have been 1948. I was fresh out of the bath and my mother was drying my slim body and tickling me. She was smiling; I rubbed at my grubby knees with the wet flannel she had given me, but this was a vain endeavour. The dirt was well ingrained from a day of rough and tumble with the other kids from around about.

I was now a cleanish boy of six, ready for bed. My old self looked down upon the boy-me from an out-of-body perspective. This child-self viewed from above physically, and from a long way forward in time.

Perhaps I was searching for solutions through the doorway of time. I saw a soulful but content child, tired from the day, but not wanting to go to bed.

I saw nothing more.

The dream scene abruptly changed: I was an older child now. Enormous black beef cattle surrounded me. Cattle with huge heads and bloodshot, staring eyes. I was afraid. I had somehow become marooned amongst these beasts. We were in the middle of a large paddock. The cattle stamped and scraped their feet in the dust.

"Don't run or they will charge you," my country cousin shouted out to me from a safe distance. He was in the paddock too, but safely close to the fence. I was about to panic and to run blindly.

In my anguish I snapped back to the present. In the periphery of my consciousness someone was talking to me. I was being offered something. A hot drink? I was unable to reply. Was it a carer? Eventually my head began to clear. On the bedside table I saw a half-cold, milky cup of tea, and some thin windmill-shaped biscuits, each broken. Had Boona been? I was detached, fragile. I trembled. Sometime later I fell again into dream-filled sleep.

I was reversing my car down a very long concrete ramp. It was twilight. At the bottom of the ramp there was a large, dark pool. The car was picking up speed. Fine. I would slow down a little. Things were under control. I braked cautiously, a slight slowing. I relaxed a bit. I braked a little more, I slowed a little more; the pool had suddenly become very much closer, and I was closing in on it at increasing speed. I braked hard. The tyres squealed; the car veered. I had reached the edge of the pool. Inexplicably the car was still slowly rolling backwards.

The pool was full of black slime, and out of the slime reached arms. Arms of black slime people whom I could not clearly make out. Their many forms turned towards me. They did not seem sinister. They were reaching out further and further towards me. I struggled with the car gears.

I must get back up the ramp.

The vehicle was no longer a car; it was now the old Bedford truck that I once owned. The truck ground its way forward. The gearbox and differential were whining from their age and with the arduous duty. The evening turned to pitch black night. The darkness was illuminated a little by glowing red points of light. The red eyes of the slime people. The red lights were slowly receding as the truck noisily crawled forward.

In my dream I had put myself into a very risky situation, but I had overcome my difficulties. Was my subconscious warning me? Was it giving me a good sign too?

I was regaining my life. I must go on.

4

The trolley stopped again that night.

My heart, my soul – they could not take this. But the stress had reactivated my tired old brain. Ideas began to flow, perhaps helped by the supplements provided by Floral's research cousin.

Even after the bad night, I felt revitalised. I stood up strongly. I shuffled about the room. I felt steady on my feet. It would be a risk to be caught walking, I thought, so I returned to my bed.

I was exhilarated.

An escape plan in raw form must have formed in my mind during the night's turmoil. It consisted of a series of bold and brazen events, each to facilitate the getaway and to obtain the money needed to effect it. The unspecified escape destination would be offshore. Perhaps the fanciful Turkey of my earlier speculation. I was acutely aware, particularly after recent happenings, that time was of the essence.

I knew I was in the 'departure lounge' at present. I must act now. I must quickly formulate the plan and then force myself to effect it.

On getting out of the Home, we must immediately have somewhere safe to repair to. A place with little risk of discovery and from where we could prepare for the greater getaway.

My first thought for phase one was that we could use the dreaded Dead Trolley to get me out of the home. I would need Floral to discover me deceased. It would have to be at the end of her shift – better still, get her rostered on to the night shift and we could leave together in the small hours when no one was about. The old orderly that manned the cart and cleaned the bathrooms would be no trouble to distract, and probably would be pleased to be sent home early. The lazy night nurses would be sleeping or internet shopping on their phones – in any case, a large chocolate cake or a bottle of gin, or both, would keep them well occupied.

With me in the cart, we could go down to the service area and leave by the back entrance, where one of the home's vans would be parked. The keys would be at reception.

Floral would need to get some money and I would need clothes – now, I had only tracksuits and institution nightgowns. Perhaps Floral could get the use of a private car. That would be better than the van which, when missed, would see the Police notified and a search started.

Once we had left the Home we could drive around until morning and then abandon the vehicle somewhere, and if needed, take a cab to our bolthole. Where was this to be? Where could an old man and a forty-something foreign woman go to and not be conspicuously noticeable? Although, I reflected, such companions may not be that unusual in these times.

I could play the role of a wealthy old man called to the city as a witness to a long-running civil court case. A trial between the local authority and a failed construction company. Yes, that appealed. Some such boring scenario that no one would be interested in or would bother to verify.

Floral would be my nurse. My ideas were flowing. I must address my physical state. I would begin a fitness programme. At present my incapacitation would impede things, plus, this was not how I wanted to be.

Tired from this planning, I sipped water from my paper cup and, smiling to myself, slipped into a deserved nap.

Floral breezed into the room in the morning.

"Have a good breakfast that you are liking," she said, and placed a plate of bacon, eggs, tomatoes and toast on my beside table. A welcome change indeed from my usual Complan and porridge. The smell was divine. My appetite was returning.

"I've got money, Paul. Yes I have," she whispered loudly. "One thousand is. Have started hiding some money from the lazy-one and taking some from his wallet when he very drunk."

"Fabulous, Petal. But please don't get yourself into trouble. Are you certain you want to become part of this thing? It is very risky, and you are still young. I don't want you spoiling your life by getting into big trouble."

Smiling and looking straight at me, Floral answered, "I actual feel great for once, never have been more happy and I don't care what could happen. Feeling alive and thinking of a good life in future."

"Well, OK," I replied. "It's settled then. You have done well to get some money, but we will need more; do you think we can steal money from here? Do they hold cash at reception? Is there a safe in the office?"

"Not much cash I think, except maybe just before they are paying out residents' cash monthly allowance," Floral answered.

"Cash monthly allowance? Is this money delivered and then held before being distributed to the inmates?" I asked.

"Think they drop off the money from the bank on the Thursdays. Giving out the money on the Friday."

"How much money?" I asked.

"Whatever the residents are wanting, I suppose."

"No. How much money *altogether*?"

"Not knowing, but three hundred and eighty resident's money for one month. Plenty of money," she replied.

"Let's say," I surmised, "one hundred dollars a week for four weeks for say three hundred recipients. That is about one hundred and twenty thousand dollars. Wow! Very tasty! We could do with that!"

My mind was in overdrive. "Floral, can you find out what day the cash delivery is, and where they keep the money prior to paying it out?"

"Should ask my friend Angel," said Floral. "She usually on reception and is Saturday girl."

"Only works Saturdays?" I queried.

"Not like Saturday – many job does," replied Floral.

"Ah! Girl Friday, perhaps."

"Yes, being that one; Friday girl," Floral confirmed with a smile.

"I need to be going now," she said. "No making them suspicious of things."

"Indeed," I responded. "I will work on the plan. Floral, please take note of everything you can. Perhaps you can get me a map of the complex too – even one of those fire escape charts they have behind the doors would do, one showing the whole ground floor particularly."

"Bye bye, Paul." Floral flounced off, looking happier than I had ever seen her before.

I felt good too.

I began detailed planning. The timing of our escape would be dictated by one of the monthly cash deliveries. We would time it with the next delivery, providing it was soon.

We would use the Dead Trolley to transport me out, and Floral thought she could get an escape vehicle from her cousin. With Floral's cash, plus what we were able to steal, we would be able to fund accommodation in which to hole up. And hopefully enough for our further escape.

If we couldn't get cash from the home, we would go anyway. If we didn't, I wouldn't be around to go anywhere.

With sufficient money, Floral could book a good hotel where we could brazen out new personas and prepare for the next leg of the escape.

An up-market hotel would be good, as it would be socially far away from the inherent working-class nosiness and suspicion that would permeate a more down-market establishment. Floral could buy me new clothes … but what would an old man wear around a flash hotel? A woman would have a better idea. I would ask Floral to take charge.

We would need luggage, too, although that could be 'following'. Once we were ensconced in our hotel room, we would become anonymous.

We would need visas for Turkey, most probably. Would we be able to get a visa to any destination at all, for Floral? There was much I needed to find out from her. What of my passport – where was it? Could I get hold of it, or get a new one? Floral could investigate.

It occurred to me that if we both went missing, and the money too, such a crime would have us quickly found by the police. Particularly so, given our unlikely profile.

I decided to be less fanciful in my thinking and make a plan that really had a chance of working. What if the theft of the money and the escape weren't linked? Yes. The money should be taken some time – even if only days – before the escape. And the escape, for me, would not be an escape. I would die, and my body would be transported away. That, surely, was a common enough occurrence at this place.

We could incriminate others in regards the missing money too – someone nasty, perhaps Dhama or Boona. They would make good suspects; we would 'frame' them.

I liked the thought of this.

Karma.

Another thought, too – what if I escaped with Floral's help, but then Floral continued working at the home and didn't join me until a day or two later? We could then fly out as soon as she started her days off. Floral could tell her husband she was visiting her sister (who lived out of town). We would have time to get away before suspicion was aroused.

The plan was forming.

I would leave as a deceased patient, and if the death was recorded, I would then be unthought of. No one would check or care.

Floral could take charge of these matters and obfuscate things so that no one would even think of following up. There would be no need of a funeral and only my EPOA would need to be notified of the death.

There would be no trouble from the senior staff here. They were lazy and suffered from the make-no-waves attitude of most corporate employees – those who only ever thought of themselves and of their bonuses. If we were careful, we could make a clean getaway without anyone snapping at our heels.

Floral had left my supplements for me. Prompted by thoughts of my physical capabilities, I took them, washed down with water.

A wonder pill, or placebo effect?

I must concentrate on the escape. I would start an exercise programme. I would start it now. Right now! No one would be by for some time.

I swung my knees over the bed; one leg was a little reluctant and I craned it over with my arms. I paused. Everything felt OK. I sat forward on the bed, pressed my feet on the floor and rocked. I put my hands behind me and pressed on the bed as I leaned over and I shot up onto my feet. The impetus of this lunge nearly toppled me over, but I managed to check my fall and steady myself. I was upright. I shuffled ahead. My legs felt surprisingly steady.

I continued, off towards the bathroom – my only destination. I arrived quickly and sat down on the toilet. I didn't take the opportunity to relieve myself, as an empty pee bottle might raise suspicions as to my mobility. I stood up, more easily this time, pulling myself up with the sturdy handhold fixed to the wall. I shuffled my way back to the bed and sat on it. I felt good. I did the circuit again. And then yet again. I was tired now, but excited.

"My God," I said to myself. "I'm coming back."

I was now going up the 'slippery slope,' not, thankfully, continuing down it.

That evening, after my meal of curried sausages (with mashed potato and peas), which I wolfed down with a newfound appetite, I was visited by Boona for a shower and toileting. Humiliating as it was, I let her drag me around. She smelt of body odour, curry, and alcohol. She was in a surly mood, too.

I was still wet when she took me from the shower room and hauled me to the bed, which she pushed me roughly onto. In the process my head hit the wall. Somewhat stunned, but surprisingly unafraid, I stared her in the eye. She avoided eye contact, but the small violence she had perpetrated excited her, and she grabbed me roughly by the hair and pushed my head back hard into the wall. I felt the brief bite of pain, and the metallic taste of my blood. Uncowed, but with a trembling hand nonetheless, I clumsily wiped the blood from my nose and mouth.

Boona was struggling against the urge to really hurt me – I could see it in her crazy eyes. Those eyes told me she had largely lost any real-world restraint. I made eye contact with her, and she eventually regained some self-control.

What is she on? I thought. She then abruptly pulled me into a sitting position and roughly tried to dress me. Again she was fighting for self-control, and as it slipped away, she backhanded me across the face and, with a feral snarl, shoved me in the chest. I fell hard back onto the bed.

Boona snarled again and walked out of the room, banging the door behind her. The noise reverberated in my sore old head.

I lay there breathless, wet, my nose leaking blood, and with a swelling lip. For all this, lying there half-dressed and akimbo across my bed, I felt alive. And, although I could hardly believe it, I wasn't frightened.

I had lost my fear. I felt an inner strength I had rarely felt before.

Boona would keep, I thought. I now saw her for what she was: an evil, drug-wrecked aberration. A coward.

Although I knew she was off the planet with drugs and sadistic by nature, I did not think that she would be courageous enough to risk the consequences that would come if she severely hurt me. I would make it my mission to get my revenge on this human scum.

I sipped my water then shakily, and rather unsuccessfully, tried to tidy myself up a bit before the lights began their descent to darkness.

The dark came. I lay back into my pillows, hurt, dishevelled, but invigorated in some way. I tried to sleep.

5

Floral and I talked at length the next morning. It was a Saturday. Usually I didn't know what day of the week it was, but I had become so enlivened that I had a new awareness.

Early mornings, particularly during the weekend, were quiet at Winston Churchill. At this time manning was by the appropriately named skeleton staff. This meant that only necessary tasks and activities were undertaken. The laziest and most conniving members of staff contrived to be rostered on at the weekend, as they got better pay and had a light workload. Consequently an atmosphere of, if not calm, one free from constant interruption and malice, prevailed.

Floral sat on my bed facing me. I was propped up with pillows, our eyes were level.

"I'm starting to walk quite strongly," I said, feeling rather satisfied with myself. "Even after my nasty contretemps with Boona I have managed to walk for ten minutes around the room this morning. Indeed, I'm feeling better than I have in five years. Is it your pills do you think?"

"Probably is those ones, and you have plenty energy from the running-away plan too," Floral replied with a smile. "That Boona is a very bad bitch. Your face looks like has bad laceration. You sure you OK, Paul Moody?" Her brow creased with concern.

"A bit tender, my dear. Thank you. But nothing's damaged, I don't think. I haven't had a face like this since my rugby days. It's reminded me of how a little hurt can assuage fear."

We talked further about our plans until Floral's other duties called her away.

There was much more we needed to discuss, but we had to be careful and disciplined and have our routines continue as they normally did.

Superficial chat was common between staff and residents, but anything more, even a hint of friendship, would look wrong in this toxic environment. A policy of detached professionalism between us would be prudent. It would also be an acceptable alternative to the overt distain that was more the usual relationship.

Floral's small but staunch coterie of oddball friends, both within the institution and without, all of whom she insisted on taking into our confidence, had been the source of much help already. We now had a full set of building layout drawings, courtesy of the maintenance man – who was very poorly treated by the management, apparently. Floral told me he was a gentle fellow with mental health vulnerabilities.

Floral had found out how, and when, the cash deliveries were made to the home. This information came from her friend Angel, the carer-receptionist.

Her scientist relative had, in addition to the wonderful pills he provided, offered the use of his spare car. This had solved our transport issue.

Floral was frighteningly confident that her newly acquired driving skills would suffice to get us around. Clothes for me had been sourced; some bought, some diverted, having been given over for disposal to charity by a bereaved (and relieved) wife of a recently passed inmate. These clothes were being laundered and altered in the home laundry by another friend. They were quality garments apparently, the donor gentleman being a man of some means.

Floral would telephone her out-of-town sister to illicit her cooperation in regards to ostensibly staying with her.

Floral was arranging her passport which, although she was a naturalised citizen, she had not bothered to apply for until now.

Regarding our offshore destination, Floral had looked into the visa requirements for Turkey. We could get tourist visas issued at the airport.

We were making a good start on our plans. *Things are starting to gel*, I thought to myself.

It occurred to me now, as a virtually unknown old soul in an anonymous institution, fundamentally alone in this world, that life is indeed what you make it, and that in many ways, I had not made much of mine.

It wasn't that I hadn't started out well in life. I had passed the endurance test that is education, and had achieved top marks in my conjoint law and commerce degree at university. I had played rugby and cricket for the university and although not a devoted rugger boy, I had done well at sports. At school, too, I had excelled, and was always in the top academic classes. Ah the days of 'streaming' acceptability!

It was only in my post-business era that things had come unstuck. I should have continued with club memberships – the golf club, literary or theatre groups, and the like.

I could see what had happened now. In the years of work slowdown, I still had my wife with me, and as a team we enjoyed our lives – overseas holidays, walks, wining, and dining, or just the garden and a movie on the television.

Now, when I should have been on the mountain's summit, looking back across the foothills to the plains below with satisfaction and a feeling of warmth, all I could see was the vague outline of distant hills in the mist.

It occurred to me that the big picture was the best view. This was what should influence my decisions – not the minutiae of life. This train of thought led me to think about Floral's brave decision. She had, in what seemed an ill-considered impulse, swerved in her life. She had joined forces with a desperate, eccentric old man in a hare-brained mission. Moreover, she had embraced all of it and questioned little.

Turkey, indeed! Floral had the wisdom to know she need not give up, that she should push back against a life of unhappiness and desperation. She wouldn't be a star swallowed by a black hole. She was taking an opportunity when it arose, however bizarre, however complex.

I hoped I wouldn't let her down.

For my part, albeit only briefly, perhaps, a little happiness was yet to be found. Maybe even some pleasure, some fun. It also occurred to me then, that we should relish our adventure however it unfolded, and not solely focus on a successful outcome. I had adopted this ethos for much of my earlier life: *relish the journey, don't struggle towards a destination.*

6

Some days passed. Floral told me she didn't think Boona would hurt me again. She had found a way to control Boona – something she could hold against her. She didn't tell me what it was, although there was no doubt plenty of scope. "Not be need knowing," she said. I was grateful, but cautioned her it was risky to advocate on my behalf. Floral thought warning off Boona wasn't so risky, and that I shouldn't worry.

Thankfully, too, I hadn't been hearing the Dead Trolley in the night and, moreover, I was progressively feeling better. My strength and fitness were markedly improved.

We must get the money we needed soon and make our escape.

Another carer came to help me. He was Slavic and sported the nametag *Pannic.* This made me grin, and I unfortunately read it out aloud. I felt rather cheap when Pannic sighed and raised his eyes. He did this good-naturedly enough, though.

Pannic didn't speak as he moved about, and although brusque in attitude and not gentle in aiding me, he didn't hurt me. I was showered and changed without incident.

My fragility was mostly feigned by now. Pannic was a strong man and although I am tall, I weigh little, and am easily moved about. After my general 'smarten up', Pannic went off on his other duties.

In the quiet time of the evening before lights out I got active, making good use of this valuable me-time. I exercised by walking around the bedroom and into and out of the bathroom, until I was panting with the exertion. I rested and then went through the cycle yet again. I was now swoon-imminent and tottering on my legs, but still OK, my old heart thumping away and my skinny old legs atremble.

I was exhilarated.

My fitness was improving fast and I could imagine myself fully mobile again soon. It was critical that I function normally, without assistance. Being seen with a walking frame or even a stick would not be compatible with the charming and distinguished older gentleman image I wished to portray. I lay down on the bed as the simulated evening progressed into full lights-out darkness. The silent gliding shut of the powered drapes made complete the arrival of the night.

I was not apprehensive for my future. I was no longer wishing away my remaining life. Sitting on my bed in the dark I longed for the richness of music and for a tumbler of whisky in my old hand, instead of the silence and the plastic beaker of water that I had.

Perhaps soon.

I closed my old eyes and mentally continued with the planning that would be vital to our success. I could look old out there in the world, but I must look distinguished too. Old and distinguished was always acceptable. My demeanour must be confident and authoritative, with a slight air of superiority. Not arrogance. A *commanding* air.

I'd need to communicate with hotel staff and other functionaries we might encounter. In dealing with these outside people (in my head I called them Muggles, as per the Harry Potter stories I'd so enjoyed some years ago) I'd need a deep, metred, voice.

At the hotel I would enquire about the food, saying I had particular dietary needs. Not silly, trendy needs, but those plausible for an old man with fragile health. Could they provide room service meals such as poached fish with a dessert of stewed fruit? Could the meals be unseasoned and without gravy or *jus* (such a pretentious word). I would couch my requests a little apologetically: *I know this is tiresome for you, but my doctor is fussy about any conflict with my heart medication.*

Yes! I was on the right track in regards these diversionary tactics, and there was no need to invent verbatim conversations. If I had the fundamental script, it would infuse me with confidence and from there I could improvise.

In my mind I was transported back to my school days and the class plays we performed. I was a reserved boy, aged about twelve. I had surprised myself when I performed on stage as, when I put on the costume, I assumed a more outgoing version of myself. A magical transition indeed. A forthright boy in place of the nervous, shy one.

An element of acting is good in life, and not that unusual, I thought. If well prepared I would be convincing in my part. I had employed role playing as a device throughout my life, though not for a long time. Ah! The other lifetime.

Floral would continue in her role as my carer; I preferred this to her suggestion of general assistant. It would be easier for her to carry on as usual, and she could be herself. Anyway, she had a natural self-assurance and would not project uncertainly or nervousness. Moreover, I would advise her that she need not entirely be her kind and friendly self, but could be more efficient, nurse-like, and brusque. This blunter demeanour would dissuade friendly chat from the ambient Muggles, with whom discussion would demand obscuration. This could put us at risk if errors were made.

Physical grooming was another matter that required consideration. I thought first of my hair. Thankfully, I had never gone bald. My hair colour was OK just as it was – silver, thankfully, rather than that ugly, fag-ash grey, the bane of the elderly. A tidy middle-class haircut would do nicely: short, and groomed around the neck and ears, but a little longer higher up on the sides, and a good clean parting with perhaps a slightly foppish wave across the forehead. This style had done me well for many years.

I had found that, over time, classical styles prevailed over 'current fashion' and that there seemed to be a 'gold standard' in such matters.

Smell was a detail to be considered too. Floral could get me a subtle aftershave. Not one of these modern ones, referred to as 'men's fragrances'. These were perfumes and were in direct competition with women's perfume. No. One of the older styles, with a pleasant freshness, giving a first impression of cleanliness and perhaps a little hint of masculine muskiness.

With all this, I would be well-groomed, dressed comfortably if semi-formally, and smelling fresh. I would be the epitome of a charming elderly gentleman. A man of refinement and status.

These thoughts reminded me of my father. He was a refined man and had tendered much advice. In the matter of dress and deportment he had advised that it's always better to be a little overdressed rather than underdressed, and that posture and general deportment say much about you as a person. Moreover, if you dress and behave well, it projects the respect you hold for the company you're in. If you make the effort, they will recognise this, if only subliminally.

This advice, although received a long time ago (my father died when I was young) had stayed with me, and had served me well.

These thoughts inspired me. I was now feeling self-satisfied and was looking forward to the upcoming adventure.

Discipline in our planning, I reminded myself, must remain paramount. We must build our plan from the concept down and not from the detail up: a common mistake, as I had seen throughout my life.

Moreover, I must not fall prey to distraction, daydreaming, meandering down side alleys, as was a weakness of mine. I must not lose sight of the forest and see only the trees.

After all this mental activity I had become tired, and I drifted into a contented sleep.

"Good morning, Mr Moody!" Floral had arrived with my breakfast tray.

"Ah, Floral, good morning my dear," I responded. "I've been doing much mental planning. Did you know you are to become an actress? Yes, an actress, just like a wonderful Hollywood starlet. And our big adventure shall unfold spectacularly, just like the plot of a blockbuster movie."

Floral looked at me, smiling. Her eyebrows rose and her look became quizzical as I continued: "There are some upcoming situations – not so very many, but a few – which we should practise, so as to make our presence, or should I say *parts*, in the real world, completely credible and above question."

My little ramble was interrupted when the door to my room flew open. Floral had left it ajar, as was the general practice of carers, although strictly speaking this was against official protocol.

In strode Dhama with his entourage. What a buffoon this man was, even more so in that he needed these reinforcements to command any semblance of authority.

My look of disdain was returned with a slack-jawed frown.

"Feeble cretin," I soundlessly mouthed.

Floral, who had been about to sit on the side of my bed, quickly leaned forward and roughly grabbed me by my chin.

"Moody," she snapped at me. "Your food is everywhere! You grotty man."

On this prompting I immediately picked up a slice of toast and jam from the small plate on my tray and shakily pushed it into the side of my mouth, moving in jerks. This resulted in the smearing of my cheeks with butter and jam. I chomped noisily on the part of the toast I had got into my mouth, and sneered at Floral.

Dhama moved to stand beside the bed. "Moody," he began loudly, as if addressing one of the blank-eyed Alzheimer patents, "soons we be moving you to full-care, security, share ward. This is due to limits of your fundings and as you lessen of mobility. No need you being taking up single room. You probably not understands this anysway."

In response I lolled slightly to one side, opened my eyes wide, and made the sort of sound a cat makes when someone stands on its tail: "YEEEOWW." I could barely contain a smirk.

Dhama regarded me with total disgust. "Brain being fully gone," he spat towards Floral. Then he nodded to her sympathetically before turning with a practised, militarily affected heel-and-toe turn, and left, followed by the other two equally overweight, rheumy eyed, caricature warriors.

We were left silent and grinning at each other, cautiously repressing our mirth (born of both humour and of relief). Then, when it was safe to do so, we began to laugh.

That night I fought for my life.

I exercised as usual, and a little later ate my dinner of curried sausages and mashed potatoes followed by a pottle of mango ice-cream. Quite a nice meal for a change.

At lights out I lay back in my bed and quickly fell asleep.

In the early hours of the morning, I awoke abruptly. There were noises at my door – it sounded as if someone was trying to unlock it and couldn't find the right key.

There were scrapings, whispers and mutterings, followed by expletives. I quickly got out of bed. Fear gripped me. *I'll lock myself in the bathroom*, I thought. I quickly moved into the bathroom. It was dark. Panic was starting to well up within me. There was only one reason they were coming now. I fought for composure: I must remain clearheaded and calm.

I must remain calm, I silently repeated to myself. Trembling, I clicked the lock. But was it locked? I tried the door to check. It opened. I could hear the key turning in the room lock. I pulled the bathroom door closed again and locked it, checked – this time it had worked. But I knew there was a sort of screwdriver slot on the other side of the door, which meant it could be opened in emergencies.

I could hear muffled, indistinct voices now. There were at least two of them. I didn't recognise them, but they sounded educated, male.

Someone half-heartedly kicked at the bathroom door. Thankfully it was a robust door. *They don't want to risk making too much noise*, I thought. My heart was pounding, my head was pounding. *Think! Think!*

I did think.

There was a sprinkler in the ceiling – perhaps if I broke that, then the fire alarm would sound and scare them off.

They were rattling the bathroom door now. I could hear scraping around the lock. "Open the door, Moody. Come out. We want to help you," said a voice. Surely it wasn't Trumpeter, the facility doctor? It sounded like him.

I picked up the metal shower stool and moved it close to the toilet. I had now regained some presence of mind. I grabbed hold of the support rail and hauled myself to stand on the toilet seat.

Teetering at first but then gaining my balance, I reached down and with my other hand, gripped the edge of the stool, thanking God for the handrail. I lifted the stool up, hoping I would be able to reach the glass bulb of the fire sprinkler.

Someone kicked the door again – hard, this time. More swearing ensued. *Surely this can't be the medical staff*, I thought. More scraping around the lock. I was reasonably steady, standing on the toilet, swaying just a little. My thoughts were now clear. There was a small window in the room – I would break that as well as the sprinkler, if I could manage it. The window was just beside me. I swung the stool at it, the window smashed making a loud, violent, crash in the still night.

The bathroom door burst open. I swung the stool at the water sprinkler above me. Direct hit! It smashed, but my momentum carried me off my perch and I fell. I crashed into the wall and then fell onto the floor.

There were two men in the room; I could see their trouser legs and sneakered feet. Water was spraying everywhere from the fire sprinkler. No alarm sounded. I was hauled to my feet. It was that bastard doctor – Trumpeter.

Finally, the alarm sounded.

The noise was very loud indeed: an alternating electronic tone of urgency.

"Jesus Christ! Let's get out of here," said the doctor to his accomplice. They ran from the room and down the corridor, leaving behind a trail of water and wet footprints.

I was bleeding from my head but felt no pain there or anywhere else. One of my legs was jammed behind the toilet bowl and the other was on the opposite side of it.

I was lying on my right-hand side against the wall with my neck bent and my head down hard against my chest. From my position on the floor, I could see across the room to the doorway. In a matter of seconds two people appeared in the doorway, one in a crisp white uniform. This would be the night nurse, I thought. The other, a large, dark-skinned man in a dark uniform, was presumably the security man.

"Holy hell!" said the security man. He walked into the deluge of water without a second thought and stooped over me, exclaiming, "The poor old bugger – he'll have broken everything."

"I'm compos mentis," I shouted at him, hoping my voice would rise above the relentless oscillating blare of the alarm. "Help me to get up, please."

They couldn't hear what I was saying.

The nurse joined the security man under the deluge. They kneeled beside me. The nurse gently and quickly examined me as best she could. The water sprinkler continued to rain down heavily over the three of us, although now I was somewhat sheltered by them.

"Can you carefully slide him out?" said the nurse to the security man.

He stooped down and basically picked me up from around the toilet, then took me into bedroom as water dripped from us both.

"Are you in pain? Is anything hurting?" asked the nurse.

"No," I truthfully replied.

Together, they gently laid me down on the bed.

Several firefighters had arrived in the room and perhaps there were other people too. There were shouted conversations. Soon, the alarm stopped and the deluge of water in the bathroom stopped too. I guess a fire alarm at an aged care facility dictates a major response from the Fire Service. That certainly seemed to have happened.

I was totally done in. I felt injured, exhausted, frail, and old. I started shaking. And then the pain began.

7

I remember nothing until the next morning when I awoke. As was only to be expected in the aftermath of that adrenaline-fuelled drama, I felt totally drained. I was heavy-headed and sore; fragile and confused.

Although the events of the previous night seemed unbelievable, they were clear in my mind.

A nurse told me I'd been moved to a new room, near to the old one. It looked identical. The emergency service folk had melted away. No doubt their reports, and those by the rest home staff, were being submitted at this very moment. Amazingly no one asked *me* what had happened. The assumption would be it was just an old man running amok in the middle of the night.

What had the nurse and the security man said to the authorities and the management, I wondered. Maybe everyone would keep their heads down. Surely such incidents weren't usual. The staff involved would no doubt be worried about their residency applications and work permits, as was the case with many rest home employees, and wouldn't want to jeopardise their chances.

Whatever, I was still alive, and although bruised and bandaged I was apparently without damage other than these superficial injuries. I wouldn't be so lucky if it happened again. We must make our move. Next time, they would surely succeed, and I would get my syringe of sedative followed by the morphine pump. Of this I was now very, very sure.

In the early afternoon, Floral arrived. "Mine God!" she cried. "They trying to kill you for certain. I only am coming now because of a very big staff meeting and talking about you going crazy, and when they call the doctor you attacking him and you are smashing up things. Dhama saying you may be very old but people like you become very strong when going crazy and that you are a troublemaker. Bloody Them! Are you very badly hurt, poor Paul? I am worry sick when hearing about all this, and not able to do anything. I am here now."

"Down but not out, sweet thing," I replied, rather unconvincingly. "Those turkeys may have tried to kill me, but I defeated the scum. Sadly, though, I am very sore and not feeling at all strong, and certainly not so cocksure of myself, and I fear for our plans. Perhaps I've been deluding both of us. I really am a silly old man, my dear. I feel I have been leading you up the garden path with my crazy imaginings."

"Don't be talking like this, Paul Moody," interrupted Floral. "We have the plan and it is very good one. We can go soon. You are hurt but should be OK in one, two days' time. Then we go. I am wanting this too and they be killing you soon if we not go.

"I am getting Pannic to watch for you tonight. Also, Paul, money comes tomorrow and I am thinking up clever idea for stealing it." Floral's lecture ended.

"Yes," I agreed. "You are right. I will garner my strength. We must follow through. I don't think they will strike again quickly – it would be most questionable if something happened to me in the next few days. You must arrange annual leave for your trip, Floral. Then, when you're ostensibly away on leave, I can take the money. After that we will wait a day or two to let things die down and then we go. We can do this, but we *must* stick to the plan."

"Yes, you correct, Paul Moody – sticking to plan is important."

Floral gave me some more supplements and we spent a little time on our plans before she gave me a gentle squeeze-hug and hastened away. She thought I would be safe for the next night or two but that we should take precautions. Pannic would be on duty for the next few nights, she said, and was well aware all was not right within the institution. She reemphasized that he would be looking out for me. Floral trusted Pannic implicitly, saying she'd take him further into her confidence, maybe even tell him of our plans. She would ask him to be vigilant with regards to my safety.

Floral had bought me a mobile phone; I decided to keep it, even at the risk of discovery. Being pre-pay, the number couldn't be traced to anyone. She had loaded a few phone numbers into it for me too, including her own, and a number here at the Home that set off a staff security alarm and the duty nurse's pager.

She gave me some chocolate too – the lovely dark, smooth, melt-in-your-mouth type I liked so much. I asked her to get me a tool – a steel scraper with which I could disable the screwdriver slot on the outside of my bathroom door lock. I drew a trembly sketch of the tool in her notebook, and directed her to an engineering supply company.

As I lay in bed that night, trying to sleep, my old head throbbed and I trembled – the low-amplitude type of tremble that infiltrates your body and soul. A heavy sleep came eventually, and I dreamt I had died and in an out-of-body way was surveying my situation and going over our plan. In my dream I floated through the facility, gliding down the corridors in a ghostly way, viewing each room and the corridors and the lounges and the common areas.

An unseen drone. I was as of the air itself; an ethereal entity.

I traversed the route we would take through the building during our get-away. This was not an imprecise trip, every inch of every part of the building seemed clear and detailed. Was I teaching myself how to get around the building? How could I have this knowledge? I reflected on these philosophical matters even in my sleep. When I had completed my tour, I found myself back in my bed and half-awake, but thankfully, not as agitated and depleted as I had been.

The faltering beat of my heart and the trembles that had taken me off to sleep had been replaced with calm resolve, and a feeling of strength. My heartbeat was again sturdy and rhythmical.

Perhaps I was psychologically preparing for the adventure. What was the worst that could happen? I could die. But they were going to kill me anyway if I did nothing. I would be ready when the money arrived. I would take it.

I could do it.

"Only Pannic," came a muffled greeting as the door opened in the early hours of the morning. I was only half asleep. Pannic gruffly but warmly asked if I needed the toilet, and put a cup of tea on my bedside table.

"I watch for you," he said as he left. "Floral tell me about things. I help. Bad people here."

The door closed behind him, and the lock clicked. I picked up my teacup, and there in the saucer lay a room key.

Later I heard the early calling of the birds. At first just one bird, calling, calling, getting no answer, and then finally the call was answered with a distant reply. Then others joined in – more bird conversations. No cacophony, but a reassuring and charming confirmation of nature and validation of that world – the real world outside.

A harbinger of my freedom?

Floral came in earlier than usual next morning, at the tail end of Pannic's shift so she was able to talk with him.

She told me she'd been granted the necessary annual leave, and had got it at short notice by saying that her sister, down south, had been suddenly abandoned by her husband, and was now in a terrible state, and needed immediate help with her young children.

This was a most satisfactory development, I thought. Real action at last. We discussed stage one: the grand larceny. We worked on the detailed plans. Floral told me that the money, when it came into the institution, would be kept in a safe set into the wall of the manager's office. She would find an excuse to go into the office and 'case' the critical area. She said Dhama was 'very much lazy,' and would probably leave his keys lying around, as he was known to be slap-dash about everything he did. She would reconnoitre to the best of her abilities, and we would reconvene around lunchtime to discuss what she'd been able to find out. The theft of the money was crucial, but details of the execution were yet to be worked out. At the moment it was little more than a concept.

We needed to fully prepare. To try and get a safe key, and to find out if the safe was physically vulnerable – if it was possible to remove it from the wall. To work out how to stage things, perhaps by setting things up on a preliminary visit – a dry run, to make the real attempt go smoothly.

I told Floral about the room key and she reemphasised Pannic's trustworthiness and his support for us.

She returned later, as expected. It was about 2.30pm, and she was due to go off shift. She was beaming. As usual, Dhama had gone off to the TAB to bet on the horses and drink beer with his unsavoury mates. Angel was on the reception desk, so Floral had simply gone into the manager's office for a look around. She had found Dhama's keys in his top desk drawer and now held them in her hand, rattling them at me, a look of delight on her face.

I couldn't believe what I was seeing. "We must take a big risk," I said, "and remove the safe key from the ring – can you go back and find out which one it is?"

"I know which," she said, grinning back at me. "It being this one." She held the bunch up by a larger, important-looking brass key.

"There are so many keys on that key ring," I said, "that he may not notice it's missing, unless he needs to use it. We must take it. Take the risk. Did anyone see you?"

"No one seeing me but Angel," Floral replied, "and she will be saying she urgently called as a patient has fallen over – she will put this in logbook for that time. I must be taking back the keys soon. My idea being not to take key but just going back and unlock safe. And then you going down tonight and take the money from unlocked safe and then you can hide the money."

"Yes," I replied. "That is a very good plan, brilliant, and certainly worth a try."

It was unlikely we would be suspected – I would be locked here in the secure unit, Floral would be off site on leave, and it wouldn't be known exactly when the safe had been unlocked, which would work in Angel's favour. She too would be an unlikely suspect.

"Floral – get back down there and unlock the safe now, and put the keys back in the drawer. And wipe them too. My God, what are we doing?" I said with a chuckle.

Floral laughed too and gave me a hurried hug. She said Pannic would be on again tonight and that the night nurse/receptionist would be asleep most of the time after midnight, as would the few others on duty.

"Good luck, Paul. Be strong. God's help." Floral hastened away.

I was nervous but excited, and felt strong enough to undertake this initial phase of the plan. There was a box of latex gloves on the shelf beside the hand sanitising station, and I took a pair of these to use during the burglary. I studied the building layout drawing I had been given. I was sure I could find my way down to the reception area. I would need to manage a couple of small flights of stairs, as it would be too risky to use the lift. I could surely manage the return trip, with a rest on the way. I did a few laps of the room for exercise. Physically, I was feeling good.

Before long, the lights dimmed and the window drapes drew shut. The room was bathed in the soft light from the evening outside. All was quiet, and surprisingly I slipped quickly into a sound sleep.

Vivid, realistic dreams swept me into a bizarre and exaggerated pre-run of the evening's events. Florence was with me, young and muscled-up as usual, but this time dressed in a costume with a cape, like Superwoman. Together we embarked on a plan similar to my forthcoming mission. This time it was carried out at speed. We loped through the hallways of the institution, moving silently and hand-signalling to each other – beckoning gestures, abrupt stop signals, and patting-down, cautionary ones. We were a formidable team. I was middle-aged rather than old, and was fitness personified, loping along beside my partner, both of us moving with wonderful, athletic ease.

Our mission slid into an exaggerated, hallucinatory version of the plan, and towards the end of it I was helping a very old gentleman to escape a scene of absolute pandemonium. Angry criminals were in hot pursuit. We rushed out of the entrance doors and into a getaway car which sat, engine furiously revving, on the driveway. Curiously, in my dream, the elderly gentleman looked like me.

I knew the risks, but what was the alternative?

8

I awoke abruptly. I felt calm and had a clear head. It was 1.55am, five minutes before the time Floral had set the alarm to. I unset it.

Time to go. I got out of bed, toileted briefly, then donned the white staff coat Floral had left for me. With some trouble I put on my woollen slippers. I took the room key from the toilet cistern where I had hidden it.

I opened the room door, locked it behind me, then paused in the corridor, taking in the situation. It all seemed surreal, but I remained calm and alert.

The night lighting was low, but my eyes adapted to it well enough. This low light and the near silence reinforced to me that the institution was in deep-sleep mode, and that I was alone.

I put on my gloves as best I could and set off towards the stairwell. My soft-soled slippers made virtually no sound as I walked along the light grey linoleum. I was steady on my feet, but nonetheless ran my old hand along the wall for reassurance. I pushed on the fire door. It resisted. I turned and reversed into it, opening it enough to step through. It slowly closed behind me.

The stairwell had a sturdy handrail; I carefully stepped down each stair. One foot down, the second joining it on the same stair, one foot down again, and so on until I reached the first landing. Around the ninety degree turn and on down the second flight of stairs. I knew this time to reverse through the fire door. Unfortunately, when I stepped aside to let the door go, it closed with a faster and stronger action than the previous one, pushing me aside. I was lucky not to be swept off my feet.

Slightly shaken by my unexpected pirouette, I stopped briefly to compose myself before setting off along the second corridor. A walking frame had been left standing against the wall halfway along. Perhaps Pannic had placed it there for me. I took hold of it and continued, now supported by wheels. Unfortunately, this method was slower and it caused me to shuffle and to make more noise. I set the thing aside and continued.

We're doing OK.

My arm trailed along the wall beside me. I was secure on my feet, not panting, and felt clear headed and able to concentrate.

I passed locked rooms, heard an occasional murmur, perhaps a snore, from behind doors, although all in all it was very quiet.

Another stairway door to negotiate, and then down the steps in a similar way to before. I was breathing more heavily. I stopped for a moment at the bottom, to rest. I should now be at reception level. Through the door would be the rear of the reception room, the desk facing away from me, possibly with the night nurse sitting or sleeping at it.

I looked through the slit window in the door. I could see most of the desk. No one was there.

I needed to press on.

I opened the door with my now practised technique, but this time, having got it open, I held it in place so that I could let it close – hopefully slowly and silently, and without it sweeping me along with it.

All went to plan. I moved forward a little. I felt lightheaded and reminded myself to breathe. After inhaling deeply I exhaled slowly – the sound seemed loud in this silent place.

The dimly lit reception area was empty. I moved as quickly as I could across to the manager's office. What if the night nurse was in there? I tried the door handle; it was unlocked and turned easily. I slowly pushed the door open a little. Thankfully this one had no closing mechanism. I shuffled forward and peered inside. It was darker than the reception area, but there was some sort of low illumination.

My eyes adjusted. The form of a person was reclined in a high-backed swivel chair, and I heard the distinct, rhythmic rasp of open-mouthed breathing. Each breath was followed by a long exhalation. Deep sleep.

There was a hint of alcohol in the air.

I remained still for at least a minute, although it seemed far longer. I quietly clicked my tongue against my palate a few times, as if trying to reassure an unfamiliar animal.

No response.

I left the security of the doorway and moved forward. My senses were on high alert; I felt an acute, almost electric awareness.

I must be careful now.

I inched steadily and slowly around the manager's desk, my eyes fixed on the sleeping night nurse. I noticed a drinking glass – vodka, perhaps? Perchance a gift to one vulnerable to the drink from my dear partner in crime? The nurse was in a heavy sleep.

I could see the safe. It was close by, mounted flush and high into the wall. I crept towards it. It was a sturdy thing with a lever handle, which I tried. It was firm but moved smoothly downward, and with the softest click the safe was open. I eased the door wide back. It swung freely. *Quality construction*, I thought.

Suddenly the nurse's rhythmic breathing stopped.

I froze, and made ready to sink down to the floor and out of sight if she stirred. She spluttered a little, then her breathing recommenced.

The safe was at eye height, and dark inside. I reached up and tentatively patted down inside. My hand met a canvas bag – a banking bag, perhaps? I lifted it out of the safe; it was quite heavy. Eureka! Money, surely. I placed the bag under my other arm and felt around inside the safe. A small stack of manila folders lay at the bottom, but that was all. I pushed the safe door closed, then opened the bank bag and put my hand inside. Even with gloves on I knew it was wads of bank notes.

I experienced a rush of adrenaline. I was overwhelmed, as if I was in a dream. My heart began to pound.

I had to get back to my room quickly and keep myself under control.

I retraced my steps, slowly, quietly, across the manager's office, my eyes fixed on the night nurse all the way. I slowly pulled the door shut behind me, but didn't latch it for fear of making a noise. I knew from experience that people who are asleep remain attuned to danger. I wiped the door handle with the hem of my white coat, to be doubly sure I left no fingerprints, then went across the reception area and along behind the desk, moving as quickly as I could. Back through the door into the stairwell and up the first flight of stairs.

On the final flight of stairs, the fatigue of the journey, and particularly this homebound ascent, hit me. Perhaps, too, I had been running on adrenaline and it was wearing off. In any case, getting up each stair now seemed a Herculean task, and I had to haul myself up, pulling with both hands on the handrail. The sack of money was securely sequestered down my nightshirt.

Finally I was on the last corridor and then back at my room. I fumbled with the key and unlocked the door, then sank exhausted to the floor. I was drained beyond thought, too tired to experience any joy from the unbelievable success of the escapade.

I lay down and fell asleep, right there on the floor.

Sometime later the crash of a trolley in the hallway woke me. Startled, I quickly crawled over to the bed, pulled myself to my feet and got under the covers. I still had my slipper-shoes on and was wearing the smock.

The door opened, and Pannic's solid form appeared.

"I go off now. Check you OK." He smiled and winked. In return, I managed a strained smile and gave him the thumbs up – that wonderful, universal signal of OK, which I could now use, when words had deserted me.

"Breakfast come soon," he said. Smiling conspiratorially, he pulled the door to and locked it.

The floor-sleep had recharged me somewhat, but I was still tired. I knew I'd better sort myself out smartly, before a carer arrived to get me up.

I'd heard the expression 'hidden in plain sight' a good number of times and felt, given the dearth of hiding places in my luxurious suite, that I might apply this principle.

Consequently, I set to work with the only sharp instrument I had – a pair of toenail clippers inadvertently left behind by a visiting podiatrist.

With these, I removed the bottom of the small window curtain. The fabric cut readily and left behind a tidy but unhemmed edge, which hung just below windowsill height. I hoped and expected that this alteration wouldn't be noticed.

The hem in the removed portion of curtain was perhaps 110mm deep, and a metre long, and was open at each end. Into the hem I pushed the wads of bank notes, each about the size of a cigarette packet and consisting of a single fold of notes secured by a rubber band. The fit of the money to the sleeve was good and the result was a metre-long, flat, beige sausage.

My first thought was to use the sausage as a draught excluder and to put it on the floor adjacent to the door. I tried this, but it looked wrong. My next thought was to lay the tube on top of the curtain pelmet. Standing on the shower chair, I pushed the sausage hard against the wall. It was visible from below, but it was the same length as the pelmet, and it looked as if it were an integral part of it.

"Most satisfactory," I said to myself.

I completed all this good work in the morning, with breakfast and ablutions being the only other activity. Next, I phoned Floral, I approached the mobile phone nervously, but found it easy to use. All I needed to do was to press the side button until the screen illuminated, and then put in the pass code (12321) which Floral had, unnecessarily, scratched into the side of my hair comb.

I found the phone's contacts easily enough, and selected *Floral*, then put the phone to my ear. Ringing commenced. Thankfully my hearing was still reasonable.

9

Floral answered after only a couple of rings. "Paul, is it you?"

"Yes, it is me," I replied. "Good morning, Floral. I have the money – can you believe it!" I was a little breathless as the reality of what I had done hit home. "I followed the plan; everything went like clockwork. Unbelievable, really. It now seems surreal. The safe was still unlocked, as you left it. The nurse was asleep – possibly blotto on drink. Apparently there's much activity and drama downstairs this morning. The police are there – they've obviously discovered the money is missing. Dhama will be beside himself. No one has come around to check my room so I can't have been seen on any cameras."

"You are a legend, Paul Moody," Floral interrupted. "Are you OK after all that?" Her voice was tight with excitement. "Was it very hard doing it? I have many things to be asking you. Are you OK?" she asked again.

"I am well, thank you, my dear. Tired but well, and quite pleased with myself too," I responded. "I think we must progress things, and in regards to getting out of here, I feel it is best if they think I have died, and that you are still away on leave. Otherwise, they may link me with the missing money and be looking for me as soon as I have gone, and they may look for you, given that you should be here but aren't. So, as soon as we can, we must go. It will be less noticeable for the actual escape if you come in here – openly, as if you're working as usual. Wear your uniform, like on a normal night shift. Sometime after the late shift change would be a good time to arrive. And your husband must continue to think you're staying at your sister's place." I paused.

"Paul," said Floral, "I need to be booking soon the hotel. How much money do you think we have got – enough for the hotel and air fares also?"

"I don't know, plenty enough for those things and much more, I think. I haven't counted it. A lot, anyway – I guess perhaps one hundred thousand dollars. There are bundles of hundred-dollar notes in lots of twenty; there are quite a number of these bundles. I agree, you need to book the airfares as soon as possible. I will get the money to you tonight so you can secure them."

"Paul!" Floral said. "I will come to your window late tonight. You can throw the money down."

"Yes. Tonight," I replied. "It would be good to get the money out of here quickly. Thank goodness there seem to be no security cameras in reception or they would be in this room right now, searching it. I do think there will be cameras in the grounds, though. Take particular care tonight, Floral. Can you discreetly have a look around the grounds in the daylight?"

"Yes, I can do this," Floral replied. "Paul, you must watch the time carefully tonight. I will be coming at two thirty in the morning. You must keep awake. Then I will come back here again tomorrow night for you, and book you out as deceased in the Deaths Register and write that you have been sent to Budget Peace and Dignities Funeral Home. We do this early in the morning."

"Yes, my dear. A good plan."

We were all set for Stage 2, but we would need Lady Luck to stay with us.

I fell into an easy sleep that evening and awoke long before 2.30am. I lay in bed calmly, awaiting the time of the money transfer.

I reflected on the past ten sorry years of my life, and on how, when I'd thought I had no future, I'd squandered the ensuing months – indeed, years.

I could have done otherwise; could have been productive, engaged, and reasonably content. I might have been an active participant in life. Instead, I had been unmotivated, disgruntled and unhappy, and had become entrapped in an awful downhill progression, all the while becoming increasingly ensnared in a ghastly dependency. More and more institutionalised.

After a time, I roused myself from my introspective ruminations and checked my phone. Nearly time for action. I needed to get cracking.

I got up and retrieved the money sausage from its place on the pelmet. Then I moved the shower stool into position in the bathroom – beside the toilet – and stepped up onto it, using its built-in step.

It was easy enough to release the window latch and open the small window.

I took my phone from my nightshirt pocket and saw that there were five minutes to go.

I pushed the window open, shuffled myself around to a better angle for viewing, then leaned forward a little. I could see down into the grounds a couple of floors below. No sooner did my eyes become accustomed to the low light than I saw movement in the shadows beside a small tree, a metre or two in from the boundary wall.

I gave a couple of long, soft whistles – something I couldn't have done a month earlier.

Floral silently and slowly moved forward until I could see her. I hoisted the money roll onto the windowsill, then pushed it down onto the sloping outer sill. One more push and it fell to the ground below, landing beside the wall, exactly as I'd hoped. I hadn't wanted to risk hitting Floral. My old ears heard the dull thud when the package landed.

Floral moved forward out of the shadows. She swept up the roll then stealthily melted back into the darkness.

My heart was beating hard. I was elated. I had never done such things, and everything was going to plan. I carefully climbed down from my perch and was soon back in bed.

I lay there in the darkness, wide awake and with a self-satisfied grin on my face. It was some time before the excitement subsided and I was able to sleep.

10

Next morning a text message awaited me on my phone. I checked it after breakfast, which was served in a perfunctory way by a new carer.

The message simply said: *Call me now.*

"Paul," said Floral, answering.

"Yes, my dear, it is me."

"Last night goes good. I am making the hotel booking now. I don't think anyone saw me. I was very careful – keeping away from the cameras."

"Well done. Fabulous work, Floral," I replied.

"Today they may be searching rooms, even full-secure one like yours. Paul, you need to hide that phone. I will come for you tonight. I will get bags for us and more clothing for you."

"What time will you come?" I asked.

"Come same time as last night. You can unlock the door for me. I will bring in the cart. You will get in it. We then go in lift to the basement. Then I do the transfer to funeral home – in that book. Angel working tonight on desk and Pannic also working. Good time tonight."

I nodded.

Floral continued, "Big problem is Boona. She working tonight and having a big 'crazy' now. Everyone says this. Angel say Boona have plenty of P drug. We must be taking much care when Boona this crazy. Yes … very much care now, after I have threaten her. I need to go now, Paul. All is

OK for tonight I think; should be having some fun too! Paul, you try to relax today."

"I will try to, my dear," I replied. "I've been hiding the phone in the glove-dispensing box – I think it should be alright there, even if they search the place. When we go, I can bring it with me."

"No Paul, push it down toilet – all way down," Floral emphasised before ringing off.

The day went by slowly. I spent much of it daydreaming of times past. I relived holidays of my childhood; individual holidays that had now amalgamated into a composite one.

An old man's recall of distant times.

A boy cooking over an open fire while camping at a remote northern beach. No need of a camping ground in those days – you stopped at one of the many beaches and set up camp. Those were happy times – exciting experiences in new environments.

That particular smell of a canvas tent came back to me, as did its *flap, flap, flap*, as it gently complained in the warm, light winds. Its walls too, slow-breathing and shivering as their unsecured bottoms flicked lightly at the grass.

Details of those times seemed as clear to me now as they had been back then.

My parents would allow me to take a friend along – a chum for company. That was more commonplace, back then. We would roam and explore on our own. Such freedom.

The modern concept of food foraging was the usual thing – for us kids, at least. We ate the wild plants; often the soft lower portions of new shoots that we would pull from the centre of the growing heads. We would collect shellfish too, and cook them beside the embers of a small fire. And we'd quench our thirst from the nearest stream, being careful it was taken from fast-flowing water!

Ah, happy times; those days of barefoot adventures.

The anticipated room search did occur. Two security fellows, surprisingly puny considering their jobs and pretentious uniforms, accompanied by an unknown carer. They spent five minutes going through my room.

During the search I maintained a suitably Alzheimetic role by lying in my bed, lolled over to one side, quite still and with an unfocused stare. My head was half raised and facing outward. I uttered an occasional low groan in punctuation to their conversations. I had to contain myself so as not to overplay my role.

The search revealed nothing. One of the searchers held the toenail cutters in his hand for a time, rotating them and staring at them, somewhat transfixed, before dropping them back into the toilet bag and closing it with a quiet sigh.

When they had left the room, I resumed my reminiscing, and this, interlaced with full napping, carried me through the day.

Soon enough the evening routine commenced: dinner, and later, lights down, and then off. Now, in excited anticipation, I awaited the next chapter of our adventure. I felt a calm acceptance of the upcoming events and had a premonition that high drama might ensue, but I wasn't afraid.

I did not unlock the door for Floral.

Earlier than expected, I heard the key turn in the lock. I had been half-asleep. I sat up.

"Only is me," whispered Floral.

I could see her outline against the dull light from the hallway. She was wearing her uniform. Floral chocked the door with a wooden wedge and came into the room backwards, pulling the Dead Trolley behind her. She pressed the light switch, holding it down for some time. The room lights came on with full brightness. The lights-out programme for my room had been over-ridden.

She looked over at me and smiled. "You OK, Pauls?" Her face was bright with excitement and anticipation. She was inspiring.

"Ready for anything, Pretty Thing, as are you, by the look of things. Will we go now? Shall we get started?"

"Yes. You put on this thing; we need to do this in case anyone look at you." She handed me what looked like a long, plain nightshirt. Sitting on the edge of the bed, I unbuttoned my pyjama top and, with Floral's help, put the shroud over my head.

I was a little shocked – it had no sleeves, or even armholes, although it was a capacious thing. With a little wriggling and manoeuvring, I then removed my pyjama pants. *This will be my genuine attire soon enough*, I thought to myself. I didn't share this morbid reflection with Floral.

"I'm wearing my underwear, but have no other clothes at all," I said. "Do you have proper clothes for me downstairs?"

She laughed. "Yes, you won't be going out in the world fully naked, Paul."

Floral lifted the top off the trolley, which was at bed height. The lid was made of lightweight metal tubes with a fabric covering. It was awkward, but not too heavy for Floral to manage. She pushed the trolley against the wall of the room, and I moved across and sat on it. Floral lifted my legs up and I then lay down and jiggled myself into suitably cadaverous alignment.

Floral was amused, but for the sake of my feelings tried unsuccessfully to suppress a girlish giggle.

"You look great, Paul. But remember, if anyone stopping us be very still, quiet – they might look at you. I will do you some make-up before we go."

With a powder puff of some sort, she then made me up so that my complexion and hands looked suitably bloodless and wan.

For my part, I felt this make-up was unnecessary, but perhaps with my pills and exercise I had regained a little colour. I kept this observation to myself.

On completion of my make-over, Floral picked up the unwieldy trolley lid and, with a little assistance, lowered it into position over me.

"OK?" she asked through the fabric cover.

"Yes," I whispered back.

"We are going," she said.

The room light went out. We were on our way; the door clicked behind us.

The gurney wheel began singing its familiar, sinister tune.

We quickly traversed the first corridor and were soon at the lift. *Surely this will be easy enough*, I thought. Floral's starched uniform swished comfortingly beside me as we moved along. She briskly manoeuvred the gurney into the lift, which sat open, waiting for us. I could hear the rustle of her uniform as she operated the controls. I knew she could override any calls to the lift from other floors.

We reached the basement without interruption. The lift doors opened. We now had to travel the long corridor from the lift to the underground vehicle access. In silence, but for the squeak of the wheels, we set off down the corridor.

Suddenly there was BRIGHTNESS. Brightness, even through my cover. The gurney stopped with a jolt. Floral jerked it backwards and we began to retreat quickly towards the lift.

Floral gave a sharp gasp, then someone screamed, in a shrill, penetrating falsetto, "YOU SLIMY BITCH! THOUGHT YOU COULD SHAFT ME!"

I went cold. It was Boona.

We were confronted by that P-loaded, rabid, Boona.

I began to tremble.

Boona was violent at the best of times, but now, strung out on drugs and supercharged with grievances, she would be brutal.

I could hear her running towards us. The blood pounded in my ears. She was on top of us.

"FILTHY BITCH!" she screamed.

The gurney lurched and crashed hard against the wall. Floral and Boona were down on the floor.

I couldn't hear a sound from Floral, but Boona was grunting with exertion. There were thuds as their bodies struck the corridor walls. The gurney lurched violently again. There was more bashing against the wall and the gurney swung abruptly and began to roll down the corridor.

Floral cried out. I could hear them struggling, and the blows from Boona's fists as they landed on Floral.

I tried to raise myself up a little. The gurney swung wildly, and I was lying down again. The struggle was immediately beside me.

Floral was making a Herculean effort – I needed to help her.

Guttural noises and swearing were coming from Boona, and muted cries from Floral. I summoned every ounce of energy and raised the gurney cover, pushing it open with my arm then propping it up with my elbow.

I was about two metres from them. They were both on the floor. Boona was sitting on top of Floral, her forearm across Floral's throat. Floral was kicking and flailing at Boona's face with her arms, and was lurching her body with all her might. She looked doomed. She was no match for Boona's power. Boona looked deranged, possessed, her eyes glassy and unseeing.

She's killing Floral, I thought.

Adrenaline intervened and I managed to sit up, pushing the gurney cover aside and onto the floor. As close as I was to her, Boona did not, or could not, see me. Floral was weakening, her struggles subsiding.

I yelled out, but as if in a bad dream, only a faint, scratchy sound came out. With this feeble utterance, Boona tilted her head and peered vacantly in my direction.

Floral arched and made a last sustained effort to dislodge Boona, but Boona barely wobbled, forcing her forearm even harder down on Floral's throat. *Floral's done for*, I thought. Tears welled in my eyes. Floral became limp.

Suddenly, as if from nowhere, a male carer in white coat and trousers appeared at the end of the corridor. He sprang to life at what he saw.

It was Pannic. He began a desperate, thirty-metre sprint.

Thank the Lord. Be in time Pannic, I prayed.

He sprinted towards Boona and Floral.

Time stood still.

Boona, unaware of anything around her, remained sitting on Floral, choking her. Pannic was a big man but ran at lightning speed. As he reached Boona, he swung his right forearm and hit her in the middle of her face.

The impact was sickening in its violence, but beautiful too.

Its effectiveness was magnificent. With a brutal thud, Boona was lifted from her sitting position and thrown into the air, landing a couple of metres along the floor.

Floral lay spread-eagled, unmoving, wheezing, gagging. She began weakly clawing at the air with her hands.

With blood pouring from her nose and mouth, somehow still conscious, Boona raised herself onto her hands and knees. Pannic, having over-run the initial impact, turned and with full force, kicked Boona in the head. She collapsed to floor, but as she did so, somehow clamped Pannic's leg with her powerful forearms. With his free leg Pannic stamped on Boona's head, and then again, and yet again. Boona, with a gurgled screech, lurched forward and bit with all her might into Pannic's leg. He cried out and began pounding his fists in sweeping haymakers into Boona head.

Eventually Boona's manic strength succumbed. Even her drug-fuelled rage couldn't withstand the physical savagery being dealt out to her. She released her bite and, as if in slow motion, fell back onto the floor. But even now she wasn't done, and started getting back onto her hands and knees.

Pannic was breathless and sweating profusely. He stamped his leg with pain. "GO, GO, GO," he cried. "I fix here. GO, *GO*!"

Floral got to her feet, gasping for air and wheezing badly. "I peeing floor," she whimpered.

"GO, GO!" shouted Pannic again, and he kicked Boona hard in the head.

Floral helped me from the gurney – there was no way she was able to push it now.

"Go," she rasped to herself quietly. Her eyes were dull.

We went.

Hanging on to each other, unsteady and lurching from side to side, we wove our way out of the building. First, we went up an endless ramp, and then out through the car park.

Floral's arm was locked around my waist. We reached her car. We were in a state of collapse.

There was no sound from inside the Home.

"We must get away from here as quickly as we can," I said, "even if we only go a little way."

Floral nodded. She was in pain and in shock; her breathing was ragged and rasping and obviously difficult. There was blood all over her uniform and she was totally dishevelled.

We leaned against the car for a few moments to recover a little, then Floral grasped me by the arm and helped me into the passenger seat of the small SUV. She got into the driver's seat and retrieved the keys from somewhere on the floor. Fumbling, she managed to get the car started, and with the headlights off we slowly made our way through the car park, out through the driveway, and onto the street.

I was traumatised, desperate to urinate, and very thirsty.

I said nothing.

Floral began to sob as she drove.

"There there, dear," I said. "We are out of that evil place."

11

The remainder of the night passed in a blur. We drove for a few minutes, then parked near to an old-style pavilion in a small park. There was a dripping tap on the side of the building, and I remember drinking water from an old paper coffee cup that Floral found in the car.

Floral couldn't speak, and could take only the smallest sips of water. We both lay down in the back of the SUV. We were in shock, sleepless and silent. I was a-jangle with adrenaline. The pounding of my heart eventually began to subside.

Finally, when I regained logical thought, I began worrying, expecting the arrival of a police car at any moment. I thought our journey would end there.

To my surprise, nothing happened. No sirens, no cars, no noise, no other movement. Just the distant bark of a dog.

Sometime later, the gentle light that heralds daybreak arrived – that barely perceptible lightening of the sky. The dawn, as it arrived, was quite unlike the artificial dawn of the Home. The soft natural light enveloped us and soon became full, bright sunlight.

Floral went to the tap and bathed her bruised and bloody face and arms. I sat on the back deck of the SUV and sipped a little more water.

Floral had clothes for both of us in a carton. She changed out of her uniform and put on a smart grey skirt and a black and grey striped, long-sleeved top. She brushed her hair, and as best she could, covered her facial wounds and abrasions with powder and foundation.

She turned her attention to me, helping me put on grey trousers made from a stretchy material. (I found out later that these were golfer's trousers – they were easy to put on and comfortable too.) The shirt she had for me was also of a stretch fabric; it was silver-grey with a sheen, not unlike my hair colour. There was also a lightweight, smart-looking charcoal jacket, and soft black shoes made from wool-like fabric.

I was astounded to be dressed like a real person again, and in such a contemporary way. *These surely can't be the old fellow's clothes*, I thought to myself.

Floral, for all her discomfort, was pleased with my look and even managed a pain-infused smile. She pointed to her throat, indicating that she was unable to talk.

She really looked a sight. Both eyes were puffed up and would no doubt be black before the day was out. There was a large graze running down her forehead, across her nose, and down one cheek. The skin on the backs of both hands was lacerated; there was a shallow cut on her elbow, and her nose was swollen, probably broken. She was limping and her right arm seemed weak.

My heart went out to her. "What have I done to you, you poor soul?" I asked, and gently stroked the side of her temple.

She became a little tearful, but magnificently, I thought, shook her fist in a defiant gesture, then gave me a gentle hug, even though she winced with the hurt of it. I felt worried for her, but also recharged by her strength and defiance.

After dressing, Floral typed a note into her phone and passed it over to me: *Need see doctor for my throat and other things. Will say I have accident with farm bike, like one on sister's farm. This is risk but need to do. Will say hits tree and falls on ground. After doing this, you can check-in the hotel. I will return to the hotel later so do not need to talk to employee.*

I responded verbally. "Yes, a good plan, we certainly need to hunker down and lick our wounds, although surely the mad Boona and all the noise and commotion at the Home has already exposed us, or soon will. Anyway, we must assume for now that Pannic has managed to do something with Boona and to cover our tracks."

I will text Pannic later, she typed.

We left the park and drove onto the motorway, exiting after about twenty minutes onto an urban road. Floral clearly knew where she was going. Another fifteen minutes or so later we came to the West Auckland township of Henderson, and turned into a MacDonald's drive-through. I leaned across Floral and spoke into the microphone, ordering two cappuccinos and a McMuffin breakfast.

Floral paid the vacant-eyed girl, who passed over our breakfasts. There was absolutely no suspicion or interest from her. Having served Floral, she immediately turned away and recommenced scrolling through her phone.

Inspired by this person's lack of awareness, I thought we might just get away with this escapade.

Floral managed to sip a little coffee. For my part I was suddenly taken with quite an appetite – a hunger I had thought long lost. I slurped down my coffee and devoured my egg muffin with pleasure – the MacDonald's was a flavour burst after three years of grey food.

After breakfast we drove to a shopping area and parked beside a health clinic. I stayed in the car while Floral went in to try and see a doctor.

It was warm in the car, and with my breakfast sitting comfortably in my stomach, I drifted into much-needed sleep.

I was awoken sometime later by the car door opening as Floral returned. She was smiling and looked relieved.

"I pretty OK," she croaked. "Nothing is broken and I have prescription for medicine."

"Great. I am pleased and relieved," I replied. "Did they believe your story?"

"Think maybe," Floral whispered hoarsely, and then pointed to her throat and shook her head.

We went off to do some shopping; first to a clothes shop, where Floral bought herself a new top – one that would cover the bruising on her neck – then to a superette for water and snacks. I sipped water and complimented Floral on her smart new look. She smiled in response. We then collected medicines from a chemist, and Floral took the opportunity to stock up on toiletries for us both.

Back in the car, she opened a pill container and took several capsules, then pulled up her sleeve and demonstrated how the doctor had given her an injection.

"Not having so much swelling soon," she croaked.

I told her not to talk, and asked if she'd heard from Pannic. She checked her phone and shook her head.

We set off for the hotel. Check-in time was 2pm, but Floral had phoned, and our suite was available whenever we wanted. We returned to Auckland City via the motorway, and after about thirty minutes Floral tried out her voice again. Thanks to the anti-inflammatory injection she was able to speak reasonably clearly, albeit quietly and with some discomfort.

"You OK, Paul?" she asked.

"Absolutely top notch," I replied. "But I'm worried about you – that ghastly facsimile of a human being, Boona, all but killed you. And we'll need to tell Winston Churchill that your holiday has been extended owing to a deterioration in the situation at your sister's. You need to tell your husband some story too – perhaps the same thing. We must maintain our cover as best we can, for as long as we can, to give us some time to lick our wounds and proceed with our getaway."

I looked across at Floral. Her face was regaining its normal 'in control' expression.

"It might be best if I check in on my own when we get to the hotel," I said. "I could say that you will be along in the evening – that way we can avoid any suspicion given by your appearance or speech. Do you feel up to continuing with all this, Floral? I am very concerned that you should be in hospital."

"I have a doctor's form for X-rays, but nothing broken he thinks – I should be OK."

I nodded.

"We are doing this now, Paul, I am very sure about that. Hard part is done. I should be OK at the hotel; you can do the talking. You can tell them, Floral has a bad cold, sore throat, and I will do more make-up on my face."

"Yes. That could work," I replied. "Once we get settled into the hotel, we can have a day or two to get you mended and both of us recharged."

I was concerned about a number of things. One was that hotels usually want a credit card, and we only had cash.

"What names do we use?" I said. "They can't be our real names, in case the authorities or others come looking for us." I looked at Floral, then continued. "I suggest we use Florence for you, as it's distinctly different but easy for me to remember, and my middle name, Winston, for me, And a nice Portuguese surname like De Garmo will do well for you – it's rather non-specific – and for me, Abercrombie. It goes well with Winston and has a certain air to it."

"Yes," said Floral, smiling. "You are a funny man, Paul. We will use these names all the time now, Winston!"

Soon, we arrived at the Hilton, in Auckland's Viaduct Harbour.

Florence's vehicle was acceptable enough, so we opted for valet parking, which would be convenient for us.

A bellhop took our small bags, and I explained that our luggage proper would follow. I felt encouraged by this preliminary interaction, as the boy didn't offer or summon assistance for me, which suggested that my walking and general deportment were sufficient not to arouse suspicion

Floral – oops, Florence – had advised the hotel that we preferred to pay in cash. Surprisingly the chatty receptionist said that the use of cash was common, especially amongst wealthy Asian tourists. We checked in.

An elderly gentleman-businessman accompanied by a female carer seemed to raise no eyebrows. After all my preparation I didn't need to use my rehearsed techniques, but I couldn't resist enquiring about my dietary needs, and asking if the jacuzzi was suitable for the somewhat infirm. I asked about other things as well, all of which Janice, the receptionist, was only too willing to advise on.

With some further assistance from the chatty young bellhop, who happily accepted the five-dollar note tendered in thanks, we found ourselves ensconced in our commodious suite.

Such luxury it was.

"Never been in so nice place as this one," Florence announced when we were alone. We were like excited schoolchildren. I opened the fridge door: low-and-behold, a cornucopia of drinks and snacks. I pulled forth a half-bottle of Moet and held it up.

"Shampoo, Florence?" I asked with raised eyebrows and a smile.

"Very much like that, please," she replied.

With mutual giggling and a satisfying cloop of the cork, we were soon happily toasting each other. It seemed appropriate to feel exhilarated on attaining this milestone of our adventure, especially after the recent trauma.

We would soon be ready for the next leg of the journey – to go international.

Florence moved our flights out by one day. We needed more recovery time. She especially needed to recuperate, both mentally and physically. Notwithstanding this need, we were acutely aware that with each hour we remained in the country, the risk of discovery increased.

Pannic phoned Florence late that evening, sometime after I had gone to sleep. They spoke at length.

The story, as Florence related to me (it was becoming easier for me to get her name correct), was that Pannic had taken Boona back to her flat – apparently a dirty place in a disreputable block of flats in Massey. He'd first procured methamphetamine and a good stock of beer and whisky, and had left Boona there with her 'provisions'.

Pannic expected that when Boona revived sufficiently, she would fully indulge her addictions and remain blitzed enough to stay in her squalid surroundings for some time.

Pannic also told Florence that Boona probably wouldn't remember much of the incident; that she had been incoherent most of the time she had been with him. He had neither seen nor heard from her since leaving her at the flat. Pannic had gone to work as usual that evening, after getting several stitches in his bitten leg.

Pannic had also sent Boona a text telling her the police had been around at the Home looking for her, enquiring about 'assaults and drug matters'. This was quite untrue, of course. He'd advised Boona to 'disappear' if she wanted to avoid serious trouble, which he would be 'happy to send her way'. Pannic was hoping that, with luck, we'd see no more of Boona.

Our hotel suite was capacious, and the bed was a pure delight – huge, and with layers of softness to it. I felt as if I was floating. That first night we both slept like babies.

Florence still looked a sight with her red welts and blue-black bruises, so the next morning we ordered room-service breakfast – full English, washed down with lattes. But we were happy to stay in, to luxuriate in our newfound happy place. Heaven on the seventh floor! I had a leisurely look through the newspaper, then we started refining our plans.

Our flight was booked for the next evening, and we felt it would be best to lie low until then. We now had our visas and passports. Florence had arranged a late checkout.

We still needed to acquire suitable travel bags and a few items of clothing.

Florence thought it would be wise to vacate our suite before the staff came to make up the rooms. This would also preclude the need to interface with these folk.

The few hotel staff we passed on our way out were all friendly. The concierge arranged a taxi for us, and we exchanged pleasantries with Janice, who was charm itself, although I saw her noticing Florence's bruised face as she chatted with us.

Florence was worried she might be recognised in Auckland. I knew it was unlikely anyone would know me. The taxi driver took us to the Botanical Gardens – a place where Florence said no one who knew her would ever go.

The gardens were a delight. It was a pleasure to be reunited with the splendour of the natural world. We had a fun tour in a little wheeled train affair that drove around the paths. Later we had lunch at the café in the grounds. I suggested that if we took our time, we'd get back to the hotel at a good hour for an afternoon nap. Florence thought this a good idea, saying, "My make-up will be breaking and falling off as it is so thick." We had a chuckle at this.

When we returned to the hotel we were delayed getting back to our room due to some problem with the housekeeping, so we went to a pleasant little area in the lobby.

After sitting there for some time, I noticed a man, perhaps in his early thirties, watching us from about twenty metres away. From his uniform and the badge on his lapel, I assumed he was a member of staff, and at first paid him little attention. He occasionally looked down at the phone in his hand. After a time, he went away, but soon returned to his position standing beside a table.

When he thought we weren't looking, I felt his eyes on us.

I told Florence to discreetly check him out. She did so by absently looking about the place, as one occasionally does. When she scanned his way, he averted his eyes.

A member of staff informed us that our room was ready, and we left the lobby. In the lift, I told Florence I didn't like the look of the bloke, and thought he'd been checking us out for some reason. Florence was unworried and said it was probably nothing – just a lazy staff member avoiding work.

Unfortunately, he was not the benign idler Florence imagined.

That evening passed well enough. The following morning, after another pleasant room-service breakfast, Florence went out to do some shopping. I would relax – have coffee and cakes and nap in front of golf on the television.

Treat upon treat.

My morning tea was brought into the room by our mystery gentleman from the lobby. I didn't like him off-the-bat; he had a whiff of riffraff about him. For a start, unlike the other members of the hotel staff, who addressed me as Mr Abercrombie, or Sir, he addressed me as 'mate', which I considered deliberately rude. There were other things too: his grooming was below par, and his teeth were discoloured.

To me these things hinted at the type of person he was.

He smirked when he first addressed me: "Morning, mate. Hope you and Mrs Abercrombie had a comfortable night."

"Good morning," I replied. "Please put the tray over there. There is no Mrs Abercrombie. Mrs De Garmo is my health carer and my business assistant. My wife died many years ago."

"Of course, mate," he replied. "Excuse, sir, for pointing it out, but when I couldn't find either a Winston Paul Aber-thingy or even a Florence Angel de da da, in the phonebook or online, I thought that – ya know – we're all blokes and that. Nothing wrong with a bit of what you like. All for it meself, mate. Eh!"

He was looking at me with his head to one side, smirking, his poor teeth on full display. I could have happily smashed the obnoxious creep in the mouth.

I put a five-dollar tip on the table by the door and told him to take it and get out before I laid a complaint.

"Well now, we might need to do a bit better than that," he replied, still looking me straight in the eye with a supercilious grin.

"Get. Out," I repeated. I had opened the room door now and stood beside it.

As he went through the door he said, "Mate; attitude! We'll have another chat after I've done some more homework." The door closed behind him.

My morning had been ruined by this malignant blackmailer. We were to fly out that evening, and I wondered if he could find out anything about us in between times. Probably not, although he seemed cunning and nasty.

I was worried.

Florence arrived back, laden with some of her purchases, saying she'd left our new travel bags in the car.

I told her about my unpleasant encounter with the nasty porter: *Gordie Fletcher, Desk Assistant*, it said on his lapel badge.

Surprisingly, Florence didn't seem worried. "In Philippines this is very common. Best thing is you pay him small sum of money and tell him he greedy. He will be a lazy one for sure. We tell him we are good people and if he gives us trouble we go to hotel manager. Then you will see, he will start worrying. He will take the small money and not bother us."

I was unsure of this approach and thought it would be better to either pay him a decent sum, or just brazen it out and do nothing.

Sadly, matters escalated quickly, and we found ourselves having to take a big decision.

We hadn't considered one weakness in our plan. This was careless. We had been traced by Fletcher through the vehicle Florence had borrowed. The creep had found out through a search of the licence plate number who the owner of our car was: Florence's relative. Fletcher had phoned him and tricked him into giving out Florence's mobile phone number (we later found out he'd said he'd found her wallet on the floor of his café when cleaning up, and that he wanted to return it).

Florence's phone rang. She looked at me quizzically, unsure whether to answer it. She let it go through to voicemail. Gordie Fletcher would know we were leaving that evening, and he possibly knew who Florence was. He might be ready to make another extortion overture.

We ordered room service lunch, and it arrived promptly. I looked up as Florence opened the door, and my breath caught in my throat. Along with our club sandwiches and coffee came Gordie Fletcher. Naively, we hadn't expected him.

His supercilious smirk was larger than ever. He walked to the coffee table in the centre of the lounge and plonked down the tray.

"Fifty K," he said. "Don't know everyfing, do I? No. But I can smell a big rat and know what? Know that you jokers are planning on flying out tonight and if the airport immigration blokes find out you jokers are using false names, well! I know that your passport names aren't going to be the ones on the hotel register. Very iffy. Questions definitely being asked. Floral – oops, sorry, Florence – you probably got an old man at home who would love to know about yous old sugar daddy; Winston, or whatever his real name is. Eh, mate?"

Florence moved to stand directly in front of Fletcher. "Mr Abercrombie very important man. We can make much trouble for you if you don't go away now."

Fletcher interjected with his lazy, lispy, enunciation: "God look at you – the old goat's been knocking you around as well, has he? Look at your poor face. Tisk, tisk; That's not very nice, is it? Police and that, very heavy on anyfing like this these days. Anyway, fifty K or I does my civic duty and let the authorities know about all this iffy stuff."

I was apoplectic with rage, and worried too. I did not have the composure to think clearly.

"You disgusting, conniving, low life," I said. "Here I am, trying to help a poor lady held in virtual slavery who's been beaten within an inch of her life by a moron, and we encounter more scum. As you have us in a compromised situation, out of desperation, we will give you ten thousand dollars to get rid of you. But not a cent more. Later on, when the truth of our situation sees the light of day – as it will – then it will be you, Fletcher, that the authorities will be wanting to talk to. You horrid creep."

Fletcher walked over and tapped me on the chest with his fingers, then slowly patted me on the cheek with his open palm.

"Don't be rude to me, Granddad – I's trying to be nice to you two. Twenty K now, and another twenty in the basement car park as you drive out. Final offer, you old prick."

"Get your dirty hands off me, scum," I replied, and ineffectually tried to push him away.

Fletcher mockingly rocked back on his feet, as if my push had done something. He then came forward fast and shoved his face against mine, his mouth contorting with nastiness.

Just as he began to speak, Florence, unnoticed as Fletcher and I stared each other down, brought a clothes iron hard down on Fletcher's head. She did this with such vigour, swinging her arms up and over her head, that the iron slid off him and hit me in the chest and arm before it crashed down to the floor, narrowly missing my foot.

Fletcher went down like a sack of spuds, his legs folding beneath him.

I began to topple over too; Florence grabbed me and managed to stop me from crashing heavily, but we both ended up on the floor.

"Mine God! You OK Winston?" she asked breathlessly.

"I think so."

"Maybe I kill that fellow," she said.

"No, he's breathing," I said, after taking a moment to watch his chest.

"What we going to do now, Paul?" asked Florence. She was distressed enough to break our new-name protocol.

"Tie the filthy little creep up – that will give us time to think," I said. "I'll need to rest for a minute. My chest is sore and I feel a bit lightheaded."

Florence was regaining her composure, and she put her arm through mine and helped me to a lounge chair.

"You had better tie him up before he comes around," I said.

"No rope. What to use?"

"Cut up some strips of cloth from a pillowslip – tie his hands behind his back and his legs tightly at the ankles and knees. We must make sure he can't get free. Quickly now," I instructed.

Florence fetched her nail scissors and cut starter slits in the pillow slip, then tore off several strips. She set to and tied Fletcher up.

He was coming around, groaning. He looked a sight – blood was running down his forehead and into his eyes, which he was trying to open. They were red and glassy.

He began mouthing profanities, punctuated with threats of some sort. Florence now had him well trussed up, like the proverbial Christmas turkey.

We were worried someone might come looking for him. We needed to get him out of the lounge and into the bathroom. Florence tried to drag him, but although he was a squirt of a man, she found it too difficult as she could only grasp him by his feet. Fletcher began kicking his legs too.

"I wouldn't do that, old chap," I said. "And it might pay to shut up – we wouldn't want to have to administer you another iron treatment."

He stopped struggling.

I picked up a wool throw from the sofa. With little resistance from Fletcher, Florence and I rolled him onto it and dragged him into the bathroom.

Fletch was fully conscious now, looking sore, bewildered, and a bit frightened.

"We're desperate people, old son," I said to him. "Don't make us really hurt you now, will you?"

I put my old slippered foot onto the side of his head gently, and said, "You really shouldn't have been born such a horrid fellow, should you, Fletch? Never mind, though, if you're a good boy now, you'll live to repent and to become a better man. Now there's a little free life advice for you, son."

We left the bathroom door open so we could keep an eye on Fletch, and sat down in the lounge. Surprisingly I wasn't badly hurt – a welt on my chest and a small scrape on my arm. The coffee was still warm, and we took a few minutes to revive ourselves with it.

"My god!" exclaimed Florence, still traumatised. She looked across at me with an expression of disbelief. "What I have done?"

We must compose ourselves, I thought. Florence said we should take Fletch with us to the airport and leave him there when we left. I felt we should involve a third party. Whatever, we needed a plan.

Florence was upset. "What I have done, Winston?" she said again. "What if his head is much damaged?"

"I think he will be OK," I replied. "Yes, he may have been out cold for a minute or two, but he doesn't seem to be confused so he probably hasn't got major concussion. No brain – no pain, if you ask me. Moreover, if he becomes unwell, we can phone an ambulance and then scarper. The evil little cretin won't want anything to do with the police. He's probably got a criminal record as long as your arm. If we give him a means of getting out of this situation, particularly if it's with some money – which is what he wanted in the first place – that might keep him from going to the authorities."

"Yes, he is a bad one," agreed Florence.

I said I thought we should keep him restrained until we were well on our way and then, if we got to our destination with no trouble, we could text him the hiding place of a sum of money. If we had a combination padlock, we could leave him bound and chained up to something. And then later, by ringing his mobile phone, we could give him the combination. When he was free, we could text message the location of the money.

"Where do we leave the horrible fellow, though?" I said, looking at Florence with raised eyebrows. "We'll need a considerable head start as it needs to cover airport time, the flights, and so on. Say twenty-four hours, all up."

"Yes," agreed Florence.

"It's opportune that it is Friday today," I continued. "We can put him somewhere that won't be used at the weekend. A school, perhaps? We can get a padlock and chain from a hardware store. During the transport Fletch will need to be gagged in some way."

These were all rather brutal ideas, and I felt uneasy about what we were contemplating. It all seemed so … criminal. But we had no choice now.

Florence had a good idea. She thought we should go back to the Winston Churchill Retirement Village. She had her master key, which would get us into the laundry building. It was unmanned over the weekend. Better still, it was well away from the main buildings, was of concrete construction and would be soundproof.

If needs be, we could probably get Angel or Pannic to discreetly monitor the situation.

We agreed on this plan. Time was getting on. We would start out as soon as it became dark.

12

We had a limited window of opportunity before our flight. We must get Fletch secured in the laundry quickly. We would send him a text message just before he became free, telling him where five thousand dollars was hidden.

To move Fletch, Florence came up with a brilliant idea: she would put on her carer's uniform, then she would look like one of the hotel housekeeping staff. We would put our luggage on a bellhop's trolley, go to the lift with Fletch, who would hobbled but able to shuffle a bit, and get him into the back of the lift where he would be hidden by the trolley and ourselves.

The lift would be full, and no one could join us.

As it eventuated, we changed the plan, deciding to take Fletch the twenty metres to the lift on the trolley. With minimal cooperation from him, we got him onto its low base. I told him that if he behaved, he would be freed after we had escaped, but if he tried to thwart our plans then he would be incapacitated. Whether or not he believed we would hurt him, I don't know, but he was reasonably compliant. He was afraid – I could see it in his eyes. Those eyes which, whilst having regained their usual shiftiness, were far less assured than they had been at the outset.

Creeps are often cowards, I thought to myself.

We set off for the lift, and then someone appeared out of a room just metres away from ours – an immaculately dressed, young Chinese woman. We must have looked a complete shambles.

"Can I get some help for you?" she asked, her eyes wide open.

"*Harrggg,*" groaned Fletch from under the woollen throw covering him. We had given him a cowboy-movie-type gag, made from a strip of our sacrificial pillow slip.

Florence dropped her carry bag onto where she thought Fletch's head was, and I nodded and cleared my throat loudly. "No, thank you very much my dear," I said. "We prefer to manage on our own – it's good exercise for an old man."

I gave her my best old-man crinkly-eyed smile. She looked straight back at me and smiled too.

"Do take the lift first," I said to her. "We will need all the space we can get!"

Thankfully still smiling – perhaps with bemusement – she went off to the lift.

Fletch let forth another "Harrggg", which prompted Florence to raise and drop her bag again and hiss, "Keep your bloody mouth shut or we be using iron again."

We moved along to the lift. It arrived back and, unhelpfully, it contained a man; a starey-eyed chap of about sixty.

"Good Lord," he exclaimed when he saw us, then he pushed past, muttering something like, "Overrun by riffraff," and set off quickly down the corridor, a strong waft of alcohol in his wake.

"We go now," said Florence.

And go we did. Our descent, thankfully, was uninterrupted and we arrived quickly at the basement. The car park had few cars in it, and we were disorientated. "This way I think," said Florence, and we set off.

Fletch was making unassertive, incoherent complaints and I shoved down firmly on his covered form. He desisted. We moved only a short distance and there was our trusty SUV.

We bundled Fletch into the back. This was done none too soon, as there were voices nearby, and a car was moving slowly down our row of the car park.

"I need to go to check out," said Florence. "You wait here, I'll be quick." She gave me a golf umbrella from the back of the vehicle. "You hit him if he is giving any trouble."

I got into the back seat beside Fletch. It was roomy. "What a nice opportunity to chat," I said. "As you know, I am an old man; my brain, though, for better or for worse, has not deserted me. In fact, I don't believe it has changed much over the years – apart from becoming rather disinterested in most things. You know, I believe I have been a good man. You, Fletch, are *not* a good man. You are a particularly poor specimen indeed. You are an expendable specimen. If you were subtracted from humanity, it would be a real benefit."

I leaned closer. In the gloomy light he looked surreal; there was dried blood across his forehead and his mouth was pulled into a slit by the gag.

We made eye contact. His were dull and malevolent.

I continued, "Of late we have come across a number of ugly folk such as yourself, but also a number of very nice folk. Ah! The contrast! It bothers me that, after we have long gone about our business, you will still be at large, wreaking your nastiness on the many good folk. What to do? Hmmm – we might tell our charming friends about you. Give you a little profile, as they say. Consequently, they may feel the need to provide you some supervision and perhaps proffer a little mentoring. You may even grow to appreciate this. An opportunity for self-growth; a beautiful synergetic convergence in your life, Fletch. Most fitting indeed, in this the age of mindfulness."

There was murder in Fletch's eyes.

"Furthermore, as a relationship warm-up, we shall ask our friends to supervise a holiday-ette for you. This wee pause in your life can be an opportunity for you to mentally prepare for your upcoming restoration and rehabilitation. Ah: personal betterment! Now, Fletch, just a wee warning. Should you not be predisposed to being born again, these lovely friends will apply corrective action. All for your own good and in keeping with natural karma, of course. One hopes any corrective actions needed would be subtle and nonviolent. Although, consensus of the circle may subscribe more to the 'blunt force to turn the brutish cur,' methodology. My goodness, Fletch, all this consideration just for you – how flattering you must find it! Yes indeed, my dear little blackmailer."

Florence was back at the car, her complexion flushed. "What you doing in the back of the car?" she asked.

"I'm having a charming tête-à-tête with our guest," I replied. "I think I'll stay here in the back as I'm so enjoying Mr Fletch's scintillating company."

Florence raised her eyes then opened the passenger door and slid in.

"Did all go well?" I asked.

"Yes, was good," she replied, starting the car. "I am worried that if we have a big problem when we get to the home, we don't have the plan B."

"Don't worry, petal," I replied. "Let's cross that bridge when we come to it. We have managed well enough so far, and my confidence is growing. You know, Florence, notwithstanding the unpleasant stuff, it has been a delight to get back out into the real world, to join life again. I've found it exhilarating. Intoxicating! Mind you, your wonderful supplements may have something to do with that." As punctuation I gave Fletch's bound form a slight prod with the umbrella.

"Dear me," I said, mainly to myself. "The absence of any power for so long, and it's abrupt return, has quite gone to my head."

Fletch gave a growl.

Florence put on the car radio. Sweet music played; an instrumental tune evocative of springtime. We exited the basement and entered the street. I was feeling euphoric, but suspected this may have been a manic reaction to the preceding events. Whatever the reason, it was fabulous to bask in life.

Florence was humming along with the music too. It was all nice, although looking back, it was bizarre that we, as escapees, burglars, and kidnappers, should be feeling this happy and righteous.

We parked up the road from the home, in sight of its illuminated entranceway.

"We will stay here watching for minute," Florence said.

"What a very good driver you are, and a skilled tactician too," I replied.

"Thank you."

"What do you reckon?" I said. "Do we just drive down to the utilities block; lights on, brazen – as if we were a couple of tradesmen called out after hours for maintenance? The Muggles will probably know no difference and wouldn't care anyway, I shouldn't think? Would you have paid any attention if you were working on night shift?"

"No, would not," Florence said, smiling at me. "You are right, Mr Abercrombie."

She flicked on the lights and we pulled out from the curb. She drove along the street and turned confidently into the main entranceway and on down the driveway. We drove, brazenly, right under the reception canopy and then at a moderately aggressive speed – as a tradesman with their inherent attitude might – through the car park to the laundry block.

The entrance was to the rear. It was secluded there. The area was bathed in the dull orange glow of security lighting. It was still and stark, beautiful – in a Kafkaesque way.

Florence stopped in front of the large roller door. She got out and went to a keypad, entered a code, opened the man-door, and went inside.

A flickering light spilled out as the large roller door began to rise. Florence came out, ducking under the door. She got back into the car and drove into the building.

We were in a brightly lit, spacious, open area. It was clean and tidy and had a pale grey painted floor. It was deserted. To our left was a wall from which issued a muffled noise.

Probably a machine room. To our right was a long counter with a hardwood top. Blue laundry bags were scattered along and around it. Life suspended.

The place smelled like a laundry – a strong washing powder smell which wasn't unpleasant. Florence pushed a button and the big roller door lowered quietly. She took my arm and helped me out of the SUV.

From the back of the vehicle Florence took the bag containing the chain and locks. She gave this to me.

"Get out," Florence said to Fletch. He glared at her and didn't move. Florence went over to the wall and took hold of a broom that was leaning there. Without saying anything further she hit Fletch hard on the side of his face.

The blow hurt; he was shocked, his returning confidence snuffed out. He began shuffling with his bottom and bound feet until he had worked his way across the seat. Florence raised the broom, and he slithered further forward and dropped to the floor.

"Hop," I said to him.

Florence raised the broom handle and hissed. Fletch began hopping – awkwardly, as one might in a sack race. It took him several minutes to move through to the machine room. This tired him, and he was panting around his gag.

We were all startled when an air compressor suddenly erupted into noisy life. We carried on further and entered a storage area. Piled beside the wall was a low stack of large sacks. Florence pointed to these and Fletch flopped down onto them and lay there on his side.

Florence moved forward and checked his bindings. She put a length of chain around Fletch's legs and padlocked it so it was firm around them. The other end of the chain went around a steel column of the building. She then repeated this exercise with his arms, the second chain locked around and between his wrists and then around the next column along.

She put his phone on the floor, close to him but out of reach. She checked the gag – it was reasonably tight, but he could breathe well enough.

"You behaving, our friends will not hurt you. Twenty-four hours' time you free and will be getting some money. You not behave, our friends come. They kill you." Florence turned. "Come, Boss," she said, and took me by the arm.

We went back through the building. Florence turned off the lights and opened the big door. We drove outside. Florence closed the door from the keypad, got back into the car and then, more sedately than when entering, we drove out of the home, heading for Auckland International Airport.

The drive took some forty minutes, and although at first I was quite distressed from the violence and criminality of our actions, soon enough the combination of Florence's smooth driving, the dark of the night, the comfort of the car seat, the warmth, and the gentle undulation of the vehicle, lulled me into an uneasy sleep.

13

In my dreams I again returned to the past.

It was more than fifty years earlier. I was on a charter fishing boat with my brother Hamish and other men I did not recognise. The skipper of the vessel was typical of the type – practical, humorous in a blokesy way, yet serious about his work, and at one with the boat and the sea.

We were well offshore and fishing for tuna. For bait we had sprats, which we took live from a bait tank set in the hull of the boat towards the stern. We were drift-fishing, and the boat was gently moving along in the sea current.

All was quiet but for the slap, slap, slap, of the small waves on the bottom of the boat. We rose and fell in slow motion with the rhythmical, hypnotic sea swells. Land was nowhere to be seen.

We had seabird companions. They sat on the water only metres from us; rising, falling, but in a syncopated off-beat rhythm.

There was no talk amongst us – we were absorbed in the environment and task at hand.

Suddenly one of the fishermen leapt up and stepped to the side of the boat. He gripped hard the stainless-steel handrail and cried out, "My God!" As one, the rest of us moved to the side of the boat which, rather than tilting a little to the side as would be expected, began to rise from the water. We were being lifted from the water's surface – the entire hull of our vessel was being raised from below.

I looked across at Hamish. He had no fear in his eyes. He was smiling, he looked exuberant. The others though, had fear in their eyes.

The boat was now right out of the water and was still climbing.

It began to topple.

I began falling from the side. My hands were firmly around the handrail, and I flipped over it headfirst. I was suspended, hanging on for grim death.

The boat toppled fully onto its side and began to slide. It was on what we now saw to be the back of a huge creature. Rods, fishing gear, life jackets, and all manner of other things were falling from the boat and bouncing down the creature's side and into the sea. Someone close to me was ranting and blaspheming in tight, high-pitched, terror.

I could not hold on. I had reverted from the fifty-years-younger version of myself to the present, old me. I was sliding helplessly down the dark, slippery surface of the creature. I looked across; my brother was sliding beside me. But he was no longer my brother, he had become Boona. She smiled at me and raised her shaved and painted eyebrows. Her teeth had become fangs.

Sliding between us was a large fish gaff. I reached out and took hold of it. I leant out towards Boona with the sharp spike of the gaff raised up. My arms, although withered, felt strong and involuntarily my old muscles rippled like those of a body builder.

I pulled down on the gaff with all my might, but as I did, I saw that it was no longer Boona beside me, but again my brother Hamish. His mouth was open in bewilderment. Just as the spike came down, I jolted awake, sitting bolt upright. I uttered a choked cry: "UUUUHRRR".

"Paul… Winston, you OK?" Florence looked across with concern. "You dreaming?"

I slumped back into the seat. My heart was pounding. "Yes. Nothing but a dream, Florence."

"You try to be relaxed now. We just had very stress, awful time," said Florence. "We will soon be at the airport and getting some good tucker and some whisky for you."

"Good. Thank you. I think I need it," I said.

I was drained, fragile, and trembly again. "Everything has been just so blunt and violent. It's a world I'm not made for, and as an old man I fear it is more than I can carry off."

"Yes, is bad stuff, Paul, but needed to be doing and he properly deserves that. We must be strong now. I upset too, Winston," said Florence.

"Yes, my dear, of course you're upset … it is thoughtless and self-centred of me to consider my old supersensitive self first, as I have done yet again."

My elder brother Hamish had died in a tragic accident when I was aged sixteen. He had fallen from the tray of a car that had been modified – the back seat had been removed, and a small tray fitted in its place.

He and his friends had been fooling around on the expansive black sands of Muriwai Beach. The vehicle had spun while travelling at high speed, or so the police had told my parents at the time.

My parents made me go with them to the mortuary to see him. I saw a likeness, but in my heart, it was not him. He was still alive.

Eventually, after a long time, I was reconciled to the loss of my happy go lucky, handsome brother. I had worshipped him when I was growing up. I carry a scar from the hurt of it, to this day. Stress and awfulness had reopened an old wound.

We arrived at Auckland International Airport. Florence pulled into a drop-off parking space in front of the terminal. She helped me onto a seat then went off and parked the car. By the time she was back I had settled down a bit and was reasonably composed. She tussled my hair in greeting and gave me a gentle smile.

"Good time coming now, partner! No more bad people or trouble. We go and have some nice food and drinks in that Gold Lounge."

"I'm OK now. Lead on," I answered with a forced smile.

We spent a few minutes getting ready to check in. A small, charming, older chap in a smart uniform adorned with badges welcomed us at the airline counter.

"Are you kids off on a party-bus tour of Marrakesh?" he asked with raised eyes and a smile.

"Got it in one," I replied. "Hashish for breakfast, lunch, and dinner." We had a bit of a chuckle together.

He whisked away our bags onto a conveyor and they disappeared off to some marshalling point in the bowels of the airport. We went through security and passport control without incident, and soon enough, after a stroll through the sweet-smelling, dazzling displays of cosmetics and expensive fragrances, we found ourselves in the hushed tones and comfort of the Premier Lounge.

It had been many years since I had been in an airport lounge, and the luxury of it was something to behold. We found some comfortable chairs in a secluded section overlooking the shimmering tarmac below, which was lined with an impressive display of monstrous aircraft.

Florence set off on a reconnaissance mission and returned to our table with two large plates of sandwiches, cheeses, crackers, and antipasto goodies. And after a second trip, with coffee, glasses of sparkling water, and flutes of actual champagne.

I immediately fell upon a cracker with soft cheese topped with a thick slice of gherkin. Heaven. I washed this treat down with champagne.

My heart skipped a beat with pleasure of it.

We had given ourselves two hours' grace to luxuriate in the lounge prior to departure. Time vaporised, and soon Florence was marshalling me to the toilets prior to boarding our flight.

On leaving the lounge, a beautifully groomed attendant with sparkling eyes asked, "Would Sir like a wheelchair for the rather long trip to the gate?"

In unison Florence and I said, "Yes" and "No", the *no* being from me. I was feeling better and wanted to walk.

It was quite a way, but thankfully there were travellators, which Florence helped me on and off. It took fifteen minutes to get to the gate, and I was breathless when we arrived.

In times past I loved air-travel, and this long-haul journey was no exception. We were in business class. It was luxurious. There was Champagne prior to take off, wonderful window views, a scrumptious four-course meal, lovely wines, and a comfy bed which was made up for me when it was time to sleep.

Kindness and attention were lavished upon us. Particularly on me. Florence, too, doted on me. Had I died on this journey, I would have left the world a contented soul. In the contrived night I slept like a baby. The fine wine and the beautiful classical music – so crystal clear in my headphones – added further to the dreamy experience. I immersed myself in the pleasure of it all.

We chased the night. It was dark outside for much of the flight, and consequently I spent much of it asleep.

I awoke before my fellow travellers and made my way to the lavatory, where I washed and shaved. Other passengers were stirring, but as the first to wake up, I was treated to a pre-breakfast cup of tea and a chat with the flight attendant, who'd already converted my bed back into a seat.

Florence slept on. I realised how exhausted she must have been, and reflected on our recent activities and the stress of the conflict and subterfuge – and, for Florence, her injuries.

She had been strong. My heart went out to my sleeping friend.

Soon after my tea, in a manner not unlike 'sunrise' at the Home, but lacking the sinister overtones, the cabin illumination increased. Breakfast was served. Florence finally woke up.

In what seemed no time at all, our miracle of science and engineering was thundering down the runway as soothing music issued forth from the sound system.

After a three-hour stopover in Hong Kong, our journey across the world resumed … and then it was over. We had arrived in the great, ancient land of Turkey.

I was brimming with anticipation to be reunited with this exotic country. We disembarked, then, after a series of careful exchanges at passport control and customs, during which Florence took efficient command, we were exiting the airport, heading for the delights of Europe's largest city: Istanbul.

"So romantic and enchanting," I said to Florence, who was wearing a silly grin and whose face radiated a calm bemusement, much like a small child might have on awaking from their afternoon nap.

"Our hotel is on seaside, Winston; this should agree with you I think," she said.

"Gorgeous," I replied. "I'm glad Customs didn't ask about the large sum of money we had with us."

"No. Maybe they just wanted to be waving on a charming old man like you, Winston."

"Cripes!" I responded. "I suppose I could have mustered up a good turn of dementia, had it really been needed. All the same, we're rather lucky pups, I think! Perhaps we'd better get cracking while the going's good."

We had a chuckle and then, with me holding on to side of the trolley, and Florence at the reins, we made our way to the taxi rank.

It was 9am in Istanbul. The weather was perfect, and in spite of the long journey, neither of us was tired.

Our hotel was an old, low-rise building of modest scale. It sat in confident, dignified simplicity on the harbour's edge.

I was mesmerised.

"Constantinople awaits you, Queen Florence," I said, as we entered our exotic new home.

14

The next couple of days went by quietly and pleasurably. We had both succumbed to mild jetlag and spent much of the time napping and lounging about.

In the evenings, Florence talked to Angel and others back home. Apparently, questions were being asked about her whereabouts, and there had been much ado about the missing money.

My demise had raised no eyebrows at all – but then, who would have cared about an ancient and problematic invalid? Moreover, I would have been considered an extremely unlikely cat burglar and escapee, so there was no reason for suspicion.

The malignant bellhop Fletch had taken his planned escape route and the monetary reward that had gone with it, and had raised no alarm.

All seemed well enough, but we knew that in using our passports and consequently our real names, we would be traced easily enough, and thus were vulnerable to exposure. We were concerned, too, that Florence's absence might soon become a disappearance, and that it might be linked to the missing money.

Boona, of course, remained a powder keg of trouble.

As we recovered from our jetlag and from the preceding trauma, we became orientated to our new surroundings. Soon we would have to plan our ongoing moves.

Istanbul was charming. It was low cost and large, but even here, in this melting pot of races and nationalities, we realised what an unlikely pair we made. Moreover, we had only three-month visas for Turkey, so we needed an ongoing plan. After much deliberation we decided it would be best to move countries again, and to do this soon.

We selected London as our destination, as it was big, multiracial, multicultural, and a liberal and tolerant place. There, I could pass for British, and Florence would meld in amongst the many different ethnicities. We would be comfortable within the western infrastructure and should blend in seamlessly.

As events unfolded, it was just as well we had a plan.

On the fifth morning of our stay, after coffee and a light breakfast on our balcony overlooking the blue sea, Florence set off to the nearby bazaar to buy our lunch – citrus fruit, tomatoes, cheese, and bread . But she was soon back again, empty handed.

"Paul; oops, Wins," she said breathlessly. "On my way out of the hotel I see Dhama and Boona. I am sure of this. They must be searching for us." Her eyes were wide with alarm. "I just kept going and they didn't see me."

"Surely not," I responded, shocked. "How could they be here? How could they know we were here? Why would they even be looking for us?"

"Definitely was Dhama," Florence replied. "I not sure if it's Boona but looks like her. They are just walking into the front of our hotel – I know that Dhama, that is him for sure."

"Shit," I said. "If they are here and looking for us, we'll be easy enough to find. This is the trouble when you have to show your passport to hotels. We need to move to somewhere we'll be much harder to find. But even if we move, they'll just keep phoning the hotels. We need a small place, a B&B or the like."

"Yes, you are right," said Florence. "We can try Airbnb. I can go on-line for finding a place."

Thankfully there was a plethora of choice. We settled on a small, self-contained suite within a larger accommodation unit which housed only a handful of guests. It was located about twenty kilometres outside the city, in a little coastal township.

We checked out of our hotel and taxied to our new accommodation, all without incident. We travelled in silence. We were worried. We were feeling like fugitives.

On arrival we were welcomed by the owner, Mrs Trevithick, an attractive British woman in her early fifties. She was warm and open and had an air of worldliness.

After the initial pleasantries she advised us that she could supply, via the small café next door, good food and coffee etc, and that we could do as we pleased while we were staying, providing there was "no noise after eleven pm." Florence, not lacking in worldly-wisdom herself, took the opportunity to explain, in her own inimitable manner, that I was an author and a luminary in alternative psychological theories, and was much sought after by groups holding alternative views on the matters of humankind (but not quite in those words).

The disciples of my doctrine, I added, were sometimes troublesome, and could be persistent in attempting to contact me. Should any of them ask for us by name or description, I explained, we would be grateful if she didn't let on that we were guests, and should let us know of any such approaches.

We settled into our new accommodation quickly and were well pleased with its comfort, quietude and charm. The first evening we sat in the tiny central courtyard of our suite with glasses of tea and red wine, discussing our situation and making plans. A small fountain played its charming water music in the background.

"We know they here and are looking for us," said Florence, adding that we should move as quickly as we could. The documents we had should be sufficient to get us into the UK.

"I will ring Angel tonight – again asking her what is happening with Dhama and Boona and the money and police things," Florence said.

She then gave me my magical supplements, which I took with fulsome sips of red wine.

We were recovering from our recent shock and, whatever happened, the place we were in was bliss. During a lull in conversation I shut my eyes, leaned back, and let out a sigh of contentment.

Florence looked at me and laughed; she was happy too.

We breakfasted the next morning on the roof top – such civilised living. How had I managed to go through life without such pleasures? I resolved to spend my remaining years at one with the cosmos, fully attuned to the soul-enhancing experiences of life. The sun was soft and warm and the food fresh and tasty.

Over coffee, Florence briefed me on the results of her evening's investigations and communications. Angel had confirmed that no insurance was to be paid on the stolen cash. It seemed, too, that there was little interest from the police regarding the theft. Indeed, they were suspicious that Dhama and Varahuchuse may have colluded to defraud the insurance company. This view was probably reinforced by their criminal histories, and further, by interviews with the staff. Varahuchuse and Dhama had been overheard arguing loudly in the days after the loss of the money.

Both had been interviewed at length by the police. Dhama was no longer seen at the home, and rumour had it he'd been sacked. Varahuchuse was absent from the place too – although this was common enough – and his sister-in-law, a more benign human being, was currently running things.

Florence's sister, Wengsley, had phoned Florence, telling her that Florence's husband had phoned in the middle of the preceding night, demanding to speak with Florence. He had been very drunk – so much so that Wengsley was barely able to understand. Wengsley, who sounded as feisty as Florence, had taken him head-on, calling him names of all sorts, including 'fat, lazy, good-for-nothing loser', and a 'drunk, violent, waster'. She had told him Florence would be staying with her from now on, and that he should forward support money immediately.

We decided to leave in two days' time. This would give us the opportunity to make ongoing arrangements.

Later that morning, drawn by the fresh air and bright sunlight, we walked along the beach. Florence, thankfully, was looking more herself by the hour – the swelling on her face was mostly gone and the bruising that remained was easily concealed by makeup.

The sapphire-blue water lapped gently on the foreshore, the wavelets accompanied by the soft, rhythmic swish of tiny pebbles. The low tidal movement had given rise to a charming, long-established foreshore area, an analogue of the alluring old gardens just beyond. Everything had a sun-bleached patina and the charm of age. Tables and chairs were set out on the paved area which ran along the harbour side, back from the sea's edge.

Florence took off her sneakers and paddled, then we sat down at one of the tables and ordered coffee and pastries. The warmth, the scintillating sea, and the hypnotic ambiance was mesmerising.

At a table just along from us, an older gentleman was drinking beer from a tall, elegant glass.

"Look at that," I said to Florence. "Beer at lunchtime."

"Why don't we too, Wins? (as she had now started to call me)"

And we did. We drank several small glasses of beer over the next couple of hours, and I must say that by the time we had settled our account and got up to leave, I was most relaxed and in a singing mood.

Not long after this, when we'd returned to our rooms, the telephone rang. It was the proprietor, saying she'd received a phone call, ostensibly from a Turkish airline, enquiring if we were guests. As per our conversation, she hadn't revealed our presence. The caller had spoken in English, she said, and had not given their name, nor revealed the reason that they wished to contact us. We felt sure it had been Dhama calling speculatively.

Whilst we were a little unnerved by this, we still felt reasonably safe where we were.

15

The next morning passed uneventfully, and in the afternoon Florence went to the airport to pre-confirm our British Airways flights. Although strictly unnecessary, we felt it prudent to be sure of our flight before leaving our accommodation.

I stayed behind, watching golf on television, well provisioned with honey almond cake and coffee. The airport was a two-hour round trip, so I expected Florence would be a while.

After four hours with no sign of her, I was beginning to worry. It wasn't until 6pm that she eventually returned. I had become a little afraid for us both. I knew that without Florence, I'd be unable to cope.

Florence's eyes betrayed her calm voice when she told me she'd seen Boona, near the entrance to the main terminal building. Luckily, as Boona had been sitting side-on, she hadn't seen Florence.

They were staking out the airport.

Florence had spun on her heel and walked quickly back out of the entrance. Then, resourceful as ever, and driven by the need to complete her mission, Florence had gone to a nearby bazaar and purchased a head scarf, such as were commonly worn here, and a heavy, dark shawl. Kitted out like a local in her new garb, she returned to airport and with a slow, slightly hobbling gait, made her way back inside. Boona was still at her post, and Florence deliberately passed quite close to her.

Florence's subterfuge was successful – Boona hadn't given her a second glance.

Florence made her way to the British Airways desk where, without incident, she confirmed all was well with our bookings. Then, erring on the side of caution, she spent some time at a crowded airport café before setting off on her return.

Boona had gone by the time Florence left.

For a while now, I had felt it unlikely that anyone would go to such lengths to recover what wasn't a particularly significant sum of money to someone of wealth. Additionally, notwithstanding the police involvement, there was still the chance of an insurance pay-out to replace the stolen cash.

As Florence sat opposite me, relaxing with a glass of rosé after her eventful trip, I said, half to myself, "What's driving this major hunt to find us? Surely not just the money – it must be costing them to send the two of them here, not to mention the loss of their time and income. Surely there must be another more compelling reason?"

"Why, then?" replied Florence. "It is only us and the money that is here."

"There must be something else. What could it possibly be?" I said. Then, cogitating further on this point, "Do you have anything else from the rest home, my dear? Keys, computer files, documents – anything at all?"

"No, not having anything else, Paul," Florence replied.

She looked through her small tapestry handbag to be sure. There was a memory stick, but it contained only personal files and photographs, she said.

"Not having anything, Paul."

"Well, everything I have is new," I said.

"Only thing I thinking," said Florence, "is maybe there is much more of their money. Maybe we should be doing a proper count of it."

"Now that is a very good idea," I replied.

We had sequestered the loot, now in a plastic shopping bag, in the small safe in the wardrobe of the master bedroom. Florence fetched the bag and emptied the contents onto the small dining table. The neat bundles of bank notes, some flat and secured in their paper sleeves, some rolled up and bound with rubber bands, tumbled out in a pile. There were about fifty bundles altogether.

"Looks like it's only bank notes," I said.

"We need to open and be checking each bundle," said Florence.

We set about doing this. After I picked up my fourth or fifth. I said, "This one seems fatter than the others – and it looks a bit different." I removed the rubber band and unfolded the notes. It was indeed different.

"What have we here?" I asked. "This is a different currency – the notes are one thousand Swiss Francs each, and there are twenty of them. Let's check out the rest."

We continued, and found that eight of the folded bundles contained a mixture of other currencies.

"The money in the flat bundles of 'new' bank notes must be for distributing to the residents of the Home," I said. "New notes, straight from the bank. And the other bundles must be day-to-day cash for the institution, or private money. Anyway, something strange is going on here. I wonder if the foreign currency is for illegal purposes. We must check every bundle and determine exactly what we have."

We interrupted our money checking to order dinner, and in silent contemplation of our new chore, we enjoyed our tasty lamb salad. Afterwards, while drinking our coffee, we set about checking the remaining bundles. Along with more foreign currency, we found a handwritten note in a language neither of us could understand. However, towards the bottom was written *USD 750,000*. This suggested the document might be an IOU of some sort.

"I'll bet this is to do with criminal drug activity or the like," I said. "But why would the note be tucked in with the money? And why would someone be so slap-dash with the security of such a valuable document?"

"These people always drinking much alcohol and doing the drugs," replied Florence, "and they are lazy-stupid. They just like my husband. You will not believe, Wins, how stupid and no good these people are. Not a surprise to me."

"Well now," I mused, "I'll take your word for it, Florence. Anyway, we now have an idea of what they want and why they're going to all this trouble to find us. The document, whatever it is exactly, we can assume is worth 750,000 US dollars to them. That's a lot of money, and it means we're in grave danger. Perhaps the note is incriminating in other ways as well. But what should we do? I suppose we could give it to them in the hope that they'll go away – which they probably would."

Florence shook her head.

"Or we can keep it as insurance," I continued. "If they caught us, that would give us a strong bargaining position. Or we can just carry on, just try and leave here, and then seem to disappear."

There was one final option. "Or we can warn them to back off and threaten to destroy their note, but add that if they leave us alone, then when we're safely relocated, we'll send it to them. We could also say we'd keep a photocopy of it as evidence, to dissuade them from bothering us in the future. But how can we contact them?"

"We could just tell them what we are doing," said Florence, "if they're waiting for us at the airport."

"Yes, but what if we get mugged first – you know, bashed or worse – and then they just run off with our things? We must think this through carefully, but I'm getting tired now. We have another day so we should rest up and finalise our plan in the morning."

Worn out, we went off to bed. But first, Florence put the interesting note inside a paperback, which she hid under the fridge, sliding it well back. Then she returned the money to the safe.

After our early night, we both awoke at sunrise. The angel that she was, Florence brought me through a cup of tea and opened the shutters of my room.

In through the open window came the soft, clear, morning light, tinged with the blue of the sapphire sea just below. The eternal sea, I mused, as it lay below me, huge and dynamic, virtually motionless, magically scintillating in the bright sunlight.

I sipped my tea and felt privileged beyond belief. My heart went out to the many other old ones that were shut up in their dull rooms in their anonymous institutions.

Presently, I dragged my mind from these thoughts and back to the loveliness of the present, and then on further, to our current circumstances and the necessary planning.

The best I could think of was, for us to courier the note to the UK, and to make it collectable only by a nominated party with suitable identification, say a passport. Florence could be our nominated party.

A movement in the bay below my window caught my attention, and I watched as a small group of four or five dolphins played – or perhaps they were fishing. They swirled in formation, in little circles.

Elegance. Beauty. I was mesmerised.

"You sleeping all day," said Florence, interrupting my moment. She stood smiling in the doorway of my room. "I'm hungry, Wins, and you need your pills. Get up, coach-slow!"

"OK." I smiled back at her. "I have some new ideas we can consider over breakfast."

We sat on the balcony soaking up the gorgeous warmth of the morning sun, enjoying fresh fruit, a light cheese and tomato omelette, orange juice and coffee.

"I don't want to leave this place," I said to Florence.

"Me not want to either, Wins." Florence looked well and happy on this scrumptious morning.

"I think we should send the note on to the UK," I said, "as a means of insurance. And we should bank some of our money so we'll be safer and financially more secure. We can try and evade the scum at the airport when we leave, although they'll probably have found out from some corrupt airport official what flights we've booked. Indeed, I'd expect them to be on our flight. Anyway, at least we'll be on our way, and we'll have a level of protection."

"Why don't we book several flights, so we are making them confused, Wins?" said Florence.

"Good thinking," I answered. "We could book two, and not take either of them, and then try and get on yet another flight at the last minute. Yes, we should make it as hard as we can for them to follow us. They'll probably find out when we've taken a flight, but perhaps not until it's left. We'll have a head start, then, and may be able to evade them altogether when we get to the UK. We could even book a flight from Ankara and fly out from there, and only book it just before it goes."

Florence liked this last idea best of all, and we agreed to do just that.

After breakfast, Florence set to on her computer. There were plenty of flights available from Ankara, and there was a bus between Istanbul and Ankara, but we decided to spend a little cash and take a chauffeured car. The cost wasn't too bad, and we'd be able to enjoy a little tour around Ankara when we got there.

We booked our car for early the next morning. Our hostess expected us to be leaving then anyway, and we thought it best if she continued to think we were leaving from Istanbul, not Ankara.

That evening Florence got a phone call from Angel. The police had been at the Home again, and rumour had it they were looking for both Dhama and Boona, and that drug use, drug dealing and insurance fraud were matters of interest.

Apparently too, after days of delay since the money had disappeared, the home's residents had received their cash payments.

An owner's investigation was underway, and management changes were happening.

Great, I thought to myself when I heard all of this.

"Surely, at least Dhama will need to get back and defend himself and protect his position in Varachuhuse's iffy empire," I said to Florence.

She agreed. Obviously, the Home was in a state, and Dhama and Boona and probably Varahuchuse too, were in a panic over the lost note. The police were investigating the money theft and other matters. We – me in particular – would be well under their radar, I thought.

16

That evening Florence settled our account at our lodgings, and the next morning we were on our way to Ankara in a luxury taxi.

I had slept badly in the night, the sinister tendrils of anxiety, ever in the shadows, nagging at me for hours. Now, although putting on a brave face, I felt drawn and raw.

Florence was quiet too. Notwithstanding our circumstances, we had embraced our seaside idyll. Moving had put an end to this.

We stopped after about half an hour for take-away coffee and pastries, which revived us a little. We quietly enjoyed our on-the-run breakfast.

In the comfort of the stately car, I was gently rocked into a much-needed sleep.

In my anxious state, frightening dreams might have seemed the order of the day, but instead I was visited by a childhood friend; a girl I'd known when I was a boy of about nine.

It was Mary, one of the brood in a large Catholic family from down the street. Mary conversed with me in my dream as the car hummed along the smooth highway, gently counselling me, a child to an old man. She spoke with a wisdom that only comes from some children.

She told me to be calm and accepting of things, and to always have happy and beautiful thoughts. I should be kind and considerate and keep away from bad people, but not be afraid of them. I should have fun, but not be silly.

In my dream I was embraced in kindness and serenity. I awoke clear headed, and ready for whatever was coming.

"You have good nap and feeling recharged, Wins?" asked Florence when she saw I had awoken. She too looked as though the gentle rocking of the car had soothed her.

We talked quietly for the rest of the journey, not about our situation, just the bonding small talk that takes place between friends when there's really no need to talk.

On reaching Ankara we felt ready to kick-on with the next stage of our escapade, so changed our plans and went directly to the airport, forgoing the sightseeing. Our paperwork was all in order, and there were no problems booking the next flight out.

Florence was able to get us into the Premium Lounge at minimal cost, and our flight departed in a little over three hours. We found a secluded alcove and settled down for a tasty lunch, during which Florence booked our transport from Heathrow to a bed and breakfast near Kew Gardens.

"Somewhere nice for walking," she said, describing our upcoming accommodation.

We felt it best to lose ourselves in London by staying somewhere peripheral for a night, and then by moving again the next day to somewhere busy where we would be even harder to find. When hunkered down there, we could regroup and plan our next move. Much like a besieged squadron between battles.

Soon after lunch I drifted off again, comfortable in my easy chair in the warm airport lounge.

Mary visited me again, and the sage nine-year-old, who in real life sadly never grew up, thanks to the polio epidemic of the time, continued her council in her wise-beyond-her-years, calm voice.

"Paul, you should make new friends and join in with things. You should do your schoolwork and accept what the teacher says. That way you will be happy and enjoy things more."

I readily accepted Mary's advice now, but unfortunately hadn't done so way back then. What trouble might I have evaded had I done so?

While I slept, Florence periodically scouted the lounge, ostensibly getting drinks or perusing the magazines or checking the departures display. After one such reconnaissance, she found me awake and said, "No see the bad ones. Only is one hour and we are going, so I think we will be OK."

"Great," I replied. "I don't expect we'll see them now either. Can I get you a glass of shampoo, my dear? I feel the need to make this journey a little party."

"Please be doing that, Wins," said Florence with a warm smile.

I was usually the beneficiary of Florence's ministrations, but this time I had the pleasure of getting the Champagne from the cornucopia of quality drinks.

Not long after this, we were called for boarding. It wasn't far to the gate, and there was no sign of the evil ones, as we had hoped and expected.

We took our business class seats and were plied with more lovely Champagne by a charming German flight attendant who introduced herself with an engaging smile as Elsa. We prepared again for that wonder of the modern world – high-speed intercontinental air travel. For many on board, the trip was a welcome separation from their daily cares and responsibilities. Sadly, one poor, misguided fellow worked assiduously on his computer throughout the flight. But he was the only passenger doing so.

Soon we were on our approach to Heathrow Airport. It was late evening, but still very light, as it is in the northern parts of Europe in the summer. The view from my window was magnificent, and with Mary's words in my ears, I immersed myself in the wondrous experience; the panorama and the ethereal awe of being in this flying community, enclosed as we were, in such a transport marvel.

We landed with the barest bump.

Florence, though engrossed in her entertainment for much of the journey, had eventually slipped off into sleep and only re-joined the world when the flight attendant gently roused her. She rubbed her forehead to reengage her mind, and looked across to me with a smile as we taxied along the runway.

We arrived at the terminal and, having disembarked, were processed in an efficient if perfunctory way. Being an elderly gentleman has some advantages, and I was waved through at every station, with documents produced by Florence whenever necessary.

I felt special, privileged, as I imagine a senior statesman or a loved celebrity might, carried along in the benevolent and easy flow of goodwill. Florence had made sure I was tidy in dress and well-groomed too – a long flight is not the most beautifying of things. I had been given a brush down and hair pat, as she might have done for a seven-year-old son, if she had had one. It was nice to be fussed over.

Our driver was waiting for us in the Arrivals area, holding a board with the name *Christmas* on it. Florence shepherded me towards him, and we greeted him with a wave. I scanned the crowd for 'the others' but didn't see them, although I was wondering if I would recognise them amongst this mix of faces and races.

We were soon out of the terminal and at the car. Not quite a luxury one this time, but it was a nice vehicle nonetheless. The air was warm although it was now well into the evening; we had travelled a long way north of our starting point.

The drive to our lodgings took half an hour, after which we received a warm welcome from Mrs Quintill, or Penelope, as she asked us to call her. She was an older, elegant lady with perfect skin and a warm disposition.

Penelope showed us to our small suite in the upmarket B&B. It was in a separate section of a spacious period home, and had been tastefully converted into a self-contained unit. Having shown us around, Penelope left us briefly before returning with a tray of tea and biscuits. Then she left us to settle in, advising us that she was at our disposal and could recommend activities, restaurants and the like, and could also provide any household services we should need.

"Ah, the English!" I said to Florence, as we sat facing each other, recuperating from the rigours of our travel.

"Very nice here, it certainly is," replied Florence. "Tonight, we might have take-aways for dinner. You look tired, Wins."

"Let's see, shall we. I'm actually feeling quite strong. I had an invigorating and insightful dream on the flight, and I'm excited to be in the United Kingdom after so many years. I'm hoping we will have fun and an adventure too."

"Hoping this part is not too much adventure," responded Florence with a smile.

After we had finished our tea, Florence drew a bath for me. I needed to wash away the trip and start this new phase of life afresh.

Having bathed and shaved, I lay down for a rest. Sleep and dreams came quickly.

Mary had become my mother – or rather, an amalgam of them both. I was counselled by this warm being: *take care, be frugal, be wise in your ways and be prepared for hard times, as they are always just around the corner.*

I floated back to wakefulness and in this gentle emergence became aware of the television playing softly in the background. I noticed through the windows that the gloaming had turned to darkness.

I dressed and joined Florence in our comfortable sitting room.

"There you are, Paul. Not feeling so tired now?"

"I'm feeling great," I said. "I feel I belong here – that I am home. It has been decades since I was last in the UK, but I still get that feeling of security, calm, and decency. I'd forgotten all of this, but now I remember. I feel we will do well here, my dear Florence."

"You are talking like poetry again, Winston," she answered. "Now, are we getting takeaways or are we going out for what you like; good food?" Florence looked happy as she asked this of me.

"I think we should venture forth and try one of the local hostelries – we should be able to find a place within a short walk. I'm not keen to mess around with taxis or the like, though."

Penelope recommended a small restaurant in the village, close to the underground station. She rang them on an old-fashioned telephone and made a booking for us. The walk was just five minutes, and Penelope furnished us with a torch and an umbrella. As it was, the street lighting was good and there was no sign of rain, but her conscientious hospitality and her warmth were appreciated.

The restaurant was small, clean, and homely.

"I do hope the style isn't the all-pervading 'fusion' food," I said to Florence after we were seated.

"You have become a very fussy fellow, Wins, now that you go business class and everything," Florence teased.

Thankfully the menu was traditional, and so, with my wonderful supplement-induced pseudo youth and vigour, I tackled a delicious T bone steak complete with proper chips and, praise be, an egg.

We chatted together happily over our meal, with which I had a small glass of Guinness, followed by a glass of claret. Heaven!

After dinner we made our way back to our new home and I went off to bed. I left Florence to study the tourist brochures and maps that Penelope had left for us.

When I woke, early in the morning, it was still dark. The bedside clock told me it was 4.15 am. I drank water from the tumbler that Penelope had thoughtfully left on my bedside table. I was quite awake, but lay back and remained still – a technique I had developed over my years spent in the old folks home.

I drifted back into a semi-sleep until, abruptly, I re-joined the world, thanks to a large rubbish truck undertaking its loud duties. I looked at the clock. It was 9.15am. Goodness! I thought.

I got up and went out to the sitting room. There was no sign of Florence – she must have been dead tired and in need of a big sleep. I washed and dressed.

There was a gentle knock; it was Penelope, smiling at me from the doorway.

"Mr Moody, I have the table set for breakfast. Do come down when it suits. I hope you slept well. Nothing is as tiring as a long journey."

"Thank you, Penelope. I slept well in the comfortable bed. I think Florence is sleeping still. She must be worn out, poor thing. I will give her a minute or two and then rouse her if need be."

After Penelope had left, I set about opening and closing my bedroom door, running taps, and flushing the toilet, all in an effort to rouse Florence. It was to no avail: there was no sound from her room.

Eventually I tapped on the door, and then opened it a little. "Florence, are you awake my dear?"

No reply.

I opened the door wide. The curtains were closed, but I could see there was no one in the bed. I walked into the room and drew them back.

The room was empty, the bed still made. Florence's bag was gone.

An icy fear enveloped me.

I dressed and went down to breakfast. I took a glass from the sideboard and filled it from a small jug of orange juice, then sat down at the small dining table.

Penelope came through from the kitchen. "Ah, Mr Moody, there you are. Can I get you something cooked, perhaps? We can offer anything in the eggs department, and bacon, sausage, baked beans, cooked tomato, or if you prefer, porridge. I'll bring through a rack of toast for you meanwhile. Would you prefer brown or white?" She smiled at me, then asked, "Are you quite well this morning? Still a little travel weary, no doubt."

I must compose myself, I thought.

"Please call me Paul, Penelope. I should like tea, and brown toast would be very good. Thank you. Florence won't be joining me; she received an early telephone call and has unexpectedly needed to slip out to meet someone. I do hope this hasn't spoiled your breakfast preparations. I would relish a very small omelette with a little fried tomato, if that suits."

"Poor Florence, having to go out so early. I do sympathise and understand. These things happen. I shall get your omelette underway. Here is a copy of the *Times* if you would like to look at it." Penelope left to prepare the breakfast.

I had seen a question in her eyes when she looked at me. I suspected my concern and fragility were showing.

I enjoyed my traditional breakfast, and began to feel a little more together and able to think. Florence hadn't gone to bed, obviously. She had left with her bag and without disturbing me. If she hadn't gone to bed, she must have left early on in the night.

There was a very sinister element to this.

She had taken her bag, but mine was still in my room. Not that there was much in my bag and, as usual, she had hidden the money – it was under the television stand. The 'note' was still with the courier company – if it had even arrived in the country. The note should offer Florence some protection if she'd been kidnapped.

If they had taken her, they would know by now that she didn't have the note with her. Presumably she would tell them what we had done with it, and that it was only she who could collect it and that her passport was needed for this. Her passport would be with her, in her handbag.

After breakfast I returned to my room and sat in an easy chair. I must summon all my strength, I thought, but strong was not what I was feeling. I was a little trembly in fact. Nonetheless, I needed to think of a plan: telephone the courier company and find out if the courier package had arrived, or when it was due? Go to the courier depot and hang around there until Florence arrived with them, then wait a bit, go into the premises and get Florence away from them somehow? It didn't matter if they got the note.

Yes. Even tell them to take the note and go away, and we would leave matters there. If they still tried to take Florence away with them, I would raise the alarm. But how could they prevent Florence from raising the alarm anyway?

Then I realised that they needed me too.

They needed to hold me as security, while they took Florence to collect the note. Having me would ensure she cooperated – they would threaten to harm me unless she did as she was told.

I am in danger now too, I thought. *I must get out of here and go somewhere I cannot be found.*

Kew Gardens, I thought. That is a large place, and it would have many nooks and crannies I could lurk in. It would do in the first instance, and was just down the road. For the directions I would consult the tourist brochure Penelope had left for us.

Now to the immediate security of our rooms. How could anyone have broken in without attracting attention?

This question was soon answered when I looked around. Behind the heavy curtains in our shared lounge was a set of French doors. The small pane of glass by the door handle, in which there was a lock with a key in it, had been removed entirely. This had been achieved by cutting out the putty and lifting out the glass, which now lay outside on the brick patio. I could make the room reasonably secure again by closing the door and locking it. However, our little annex with its timber joinery throughout, and its flimsy window and door catches, would never be secure.

I made myself tea and sat down to think. Perhaps they would contact me and make me cooperate by threatening to hurt Florence. I needed to have my phone turned on. Was it even charged? We mainly used Florence's.

I found it and turned it on. The battery icon indicated it was fully charged. I knew Florence had arranged for it to function in the UK – she had said it would work when we arrived, without any further arrangements. Presumably it would ring if someone wanted to contact me. I sighed. I was starting to feel overwhelmed by the situation and its complexity. Perhaps I should just go to the authorities and come clean.

I couldn't bear the thought of Florence being hurt, or even killed. And for my part, whatever happened to me was unimportant – I had lived my life, although much of it had been squandered.

Eventually I decided to confide in Penelope. Partly because she might now be in danger too.

17

"How extraordinary!" exclaimed Penelope when I had completed the outline of our saga. I was expecting her to recommend I immediately contact the police, but surprisingly, she had another thought in mind altogether. Moreover, she seemed unconcerned about our dubious activities, although I hadn't been too extravagant with the details.

"I think we should discuss this matter with my brother, Sedgeforth. Yes … yes … ask his advice," Penelope said thoughtfully.

"Sedgeforth!" I involuntarily echoed.

Penelope looked up. "Oh, don't be put off by his name, Paul – one of Father's silly snobbish ways. I was to be Feltham, apparently. Can you believe it! Thankfully Mother drew an emphatic line in the sand on that. Now, dear brother Sedgeforth, although he's retired, was some sort of policeman and he is the personification of the old-boy network; very well connected. Moreover, he needs something to do. I shall telephone right after I get you a calming cup of tea."

"Yes, that would be very nice. Thank you, Penelope. I feel quite shaken, to be honest."

"Of course you do you, poor dear," said Penelope as she left the room.

She returned a short while later with my tea, and told me Sedgey was on his way over. She warned he could be rather eccentric and politically incorrect, but assured me he was a good man, and a clever one too, and that notwithstanding his eighty years, he was fit mentally and physically.

Sedgey arrived. He was a striking fellow indeed – a young-looking octogenarian. His hair was still largely black, he was tall and slight and introduced himself with direct eye contact. There was a warmth, too, in his piercing blue eyes.

I felt comfortable with Sedgey immediately.

After the introductions we all sat together in the little sitting room, Sedgey leaning forward in his chair, his head cocked to the side, nodding as I retold our story.

'I cannot put at risk such kind folk as you,' I finished. 'I regret burdening you with this unwanted trouble. I think I should go to the police.'

"Not a bit of it," said Sedgey. "Can't wait to get stuck into things. We old fellows must stick together, Paul, and I must say, I do envy you your adventure. Excellent stuff; must push back against the insidious new order, eh! Can definitely help here, old boy. Used to be a policeman myself, but must say, the regular police can be a bit clumsy."

He sat back in his chair and crossed one leg over the other. "Yes, I still do a bit of that sort of work occasionally. Now! We must do all that we can to make your dear companion safe. First, we will buy a little time. I want you to phone Florence. Do it now, and tell whoever answers – it's unlikely to be her, I think – that you will do whatever they say. Emphasise that you just want Florence safely back. Moreover, you can tell them you'll have all of their money returned to them and that you will stand by with your phone at the ready to act immediately on their instructions."

"Do you think this is the best way?" I asked.

Sedgy nodded.

I got my phone from the bedroom and gave it to Sedgey.

"You may have checked it previously, but it's now off," he observed. "That may be a blessing." He turned it back on. "Hmmm – battery rather flat too. Do you have a charger?"

I felt foolish that the phone had been off – I was sure it was on, and had thought the battery OK too. "I think Florence has the charger," I said. "I should have had it charged and turned on, shouldn't I? I haven't been on top of things I'm afraid."

"Perfectly understandable," said Sedgey. "I have a charger in the car. I'll get it. Penelope, dear, can you get your power bank?"

Just as they arrived back, the phone started ringing.

Sedgey picked it up, accepted the call, then handed it to me.

"Paul, it is Florence speaking. Thank goodness I finally get you."

"My poor dear," I interrupted. "I am beside myself with worry for you – are you alright?"

"I am fine, but we need to be giving them the note that they are wanting. Also they want you to come here so I can go to the courier place and get the note. They worried I will run away if it is only me."

"Of course, my dear," I said. "I will do whatever they want."

Sedgey was pointing at the battery charger and gently tugging on my sleeve.

"Florence – the phone's about to go flat, but I'll charge it up and keep it on. Tell them I agree to do anything."

"Yes, Paul, OK. They want me to say that we will not be hurt if we do these things–"

The phone went dead.

"Excellent development – what luck," said Sedgey.

He plugged the charger lead into the phone and after a few moments turned it back on. To make it simpler for me, Florence had set up the phone without a password and Sedgey was able to scroll through and get the number of my phone and the number of the phone from which Florence had just called. The call hadn't been from her usual mobile but from a pre-paid number. Armed with this detail, Sedgey called a contact by the name of Harold, who was able to get an approximate location of Florence's phone.

Sedgey announced that the sitting room would become the Operations Centre, and further recruits were to be enlisted forthwith.

My head was spinning with all this activity. Sedgey seemed to be enjoying himself – perhaps a little too much.

Within the hour, two of Sedgey's colleagues had joined us. Rupert was a tiny man of about sixty, with smooth, pale skin and fine features, and Moose was a fully bearded Canadian of about fifty, who was quite the opposite of Rupert – big and loud.

Both men were respectful and didn't question the veracity of our unusual predicament when it was explained it to them. On the contrary, they instantly accepted our innocence, and that our pursuers were evil incarnate.

"Paul, sir," said Moose, "we'll not only rescue Miss Florence for you, but we will teach those goddam suckers a good lesson too." He was ebullient and smiley, and he certainly enjoyed the drink, as was evident when he quickly vacuumed up two cans of beer brought in by Penelope on a drinks trolley, and set about opening a third.

Sedgey and Rupert had helped themselves too. *It's not a party*, I thought. But perhaps it countered the adrenaline. Could it be their usual modus operandi?

Phone calls were being made and conversations were taking place. It seemed they had activated a network of associates.

Although all this activity wasn't particularly loud or frenetic, it all became a little too much for me, and this must have been showing. Sedgey, in his all-noticing way, detected that I was flagging and said he would bring the phone through to me if necessary. Then he had Penelope take me through to my room for a lie down.

"We'll sort those nasty fellows out, don't worry, my boy," he said.

"You have a nap, darling, and I will get you later for supper," said Penelope as I lay back on the bed.

I was soon engulfed in much-needed sleep.

I was again my twenty-year-old self, frozen in that long transition between adolescence and adulthood that males sometimes find themselves stuck in.

I was outdoors, somewhere in the South Island high country; it may have been Milford Sound, and I was tramping along a narrow rock-strewn track surrounded by thick, low scrubland. Someone was in front of me; from behind it looked like my father. Was it him? I looked more closely. I was worried and felt tired; my breathing was laboured. The person ahead was drawing away from me, nimble in movement as he bounded from rock to rock and leapt over the path's muddy patches and ankle-threatening undulations.

I was making heavy weather of it, slipping off the steep, muddy depressions, awkwardly stumbling when landing from ill-timed leaps. I was drained of energy. I heard a noise from behind – someone was following me, and they were getting closer.

I felt an icy chill.

My forward companion was now out of sight around a bend. I dared not turn around, both through fear, and because I might lose distance or worse, my footing. I summoned all my strength and increased my speed. I was half running now, slipping, sliding, stumbling.

I was down.

On my hands and knees, scrambling through the mud and stones, I cried out as I felt the weight of my pursuer land on me. I saw myself from above.

My soul had left my body.

I was awake. In my anguish I had lurched; my arm was trapped under me.

Penelope stood beside the bed. "You cried out, dear," she said, putting her arm under my shoulders to help me sit up.

"You stay put, Paul; I will bring you through a tray in a minute. You must have been dreaming, throwing yourself about. Are you hurt? Really, what an awful time you've had. You mustn't worry now, Sedgey will sort things out. He's incredibly good at this sort of thing."

Penelope helped me sit higher up on the bed and gave my forehead a little rub, then sat on the bed beside me. I was propped up by pillows and cushions, and my head began to clear.

Better composed, I turned to her. "Thank you so much. What an unwanted nuisance I am. I do apologise for bringing this trouble down on your heads. You are being so kind, all of you. I don't deserve it."

"Nonsense," Penelope answered. "You must try not to worry. When Rupert heard you were a bit poorly, he said he had a good elixir that you might take. I don't think it's an entirely a sanctioned thing, but I would take anything he recommends. For all his gentle ways, Rupert's quite a remarkable person, very clever, as are they all, and highly educated, knowledgeable. All of them are rather special. They want to help you – they thrive on being useful and exercising their talents."

I took a teaspoon of the elixir Penelope proffered.

She continued, "I'll fetch you some of my homemade chicken consommé – you'll find it's reinvigorating, and soothing too. We'll all have a little of it. Now don't think of another thing this evening, Paul. Sedgey will look after absolutely everything. He and the team are making good headway already. They're using your name for our adversaries: the EO – the Evil Ones. I do like that. One should be clear about what one is up against, I think."

I did feel revived, and I got up soon after and had my soup with the others. We sat around in the easy chairs. Everyone was quiet and thoughtful. To follow the soup, a large plate of Welsh rarebit was placed on the occasional table in the centre of the room.

When we were well into our meal, Moose turned to me and said, "You're looking way better now, Champ. We must set you a task or two to keep you busy. One thing we do need to know is what your friend looks like; a full description of her would be good. Rupert couldn't find any photos of her on your mobile or on the internet. Another thing: details of what she was wearing, and of her bag and anything else she had. We have her phone number of course – that's very useful."

"Yes," chimed in Sedgey. "Soon, Paul, we will move from our preliminary investigations and onto operational matters. We already know where the EO are. Indeed, at this instant they're drinking in a West End pub – we know the very one. Rupert has been considering matters from their perspective; he has decided not to credit them with much capability or acumen. He thinks that the best scenario for us to work from is that they know you are worried, but believe you will be too vulnerable, and too concerned for Florence, to go to the police."

Rupert cleared his throat and nodded in assent.

Sedgey continued, "They'll be expecting you to be awaiting their instructions, and we think that these, when they come, will be for you to change places with Florence. Then they will send her on her own to the courier company to get the package. When they have what they want, we think it likely they'll have you both held in some way, but otherwise won't harm you, whilst they quickly leave the country. There is some risk that they might incapacitate you more permanently, but this seems unlikely, as committing a serious crime would put them at high risk and in high visibility with the police, and would have them pursued internationally."

I nodded, but wasn't so sure they would be so well organised.

Sedgey carried on. "In any case, given this scenario, they will probably contact you soon – first thing in the morning, we predict – so that they can get on with the courier recovery. We won't wait for this to eventuate – although we may allow it to happen. We'll have them under tight surveillance. Paul – what more can you tell us about the EO?"

I explained in some detail the crude and brutal nature of our pursuers.

Sedgey nodded, and I concluded, "I believe the pair of them will stop at nothing to get the million-dollar note back. Both have animal cunning in abundance, and the feral characteristics of wily street-people. They are dangerous. I must emphasise, I don't want anyone put at risk, and although it's extremely kind of all of you to help us, I feel it would be better for me alone to just do as they direct, and hope – and I think we might expect – that once they have what they want they will be on their way and leave us be." I ended my thoughts there.

"You must trust us, Paul," said Sedgey. "We need not elaborate on our backgrounds or experience – you are a clever man, and you can extrapolate for yourself. The likes of your adversaries, in our long experience, are simply evil.

You cannot do a deal with such people. These types get pleasure from hurt and gratuitous violence. You must let us remain in charge. There will be some risk, but what we do in such situations is find out everything we can, as quickly as we can, and then take command of the situation. If we do this well, the third party are unaware of us, and mistakenly think that they are setting the agenda and controlling activities."

I nodded; this seemed sensible and likely.

"We already know where the EO are," he continued, "and we are strategizing the scenarios we wish to play out."

At this point Sedgey directed me with his eyes toward the others. Rupert, Moose and Penelope were looking intently and genially at me.

"Yes," I replied, "I see I have the A team on my side. I acknowledge what you're saying, Sedgey, and I am most grateful."

"Good," said Sedgey. "Then we will hear no more of your concerns. Let us be in charge, Paul, but you must play a vital role in the team. And the team is larger than you might think. Rupert and Penelope will work closely with you to form a platoon within the greater force. Your particular tasks will be pivotal to the outcome." Sedgey smiled and stood up. "Now, on with things. We have much to do. Penny, dear, put on the coffee. We're in for a long night."

18

I sat down at the table and wrote out a detailed description of Florence. On completion I felt that anyone at all would recognise her from it. Looking back, I realise that they only gave me this task to keep me occupied.

An hour or two later I was sent off to bed. I slept well, without the ravaging dreams of my earlier sleep, and woke very early in the morning. After lying awake for a time, sleep again claimed me and it wasn't until 8am that Penelope roused me with a cup of tea.

"Wake up, lazybones – there's work to be done," she said with a smile. "Would you like me to draw you a nice bath?"

I answered affirmatively, and after a fabulous, deep, hot bath I dressed and joined the team. It looked to me as if they'd been up all night, although they still seemed alert.

"Ah, Paul," said Sedgey. "Everything is coming along nicely. Rupert is about to put on the nose bag, so why not go along with him and Penelope and have a little breakfast. They will fill you in on the overnight developments."

I took the same breakfast as Rupert: boiled eggs with soldiers, followed by marmalade toast, and tea.

Some things remain perfect throughout your life.

Penelope sat down with us for her half grapefruit and bowl of rolled oats. After some minutes of eating quietly, Rupert told of developments so far.

The EO were staying in a small, low-cost hotel in the West End. They had rented a van, and were more than likely holding Florence in it. Our team had managed to get a stand-in maid to go to each of the EO's two hotel rooms, and Florence didn't appear to be in either.

"But how would they stop her escaping or raising the alarm if she was left out in the van?" I asked.

"She will be going along with their instructions," said Rupert, "as she will have been threatened with consequences if she doesn't, much as she has already told you. And they probably have a minder with her."

Rupert also relayed that the EO had flown in from Turkey about four hours behind Florence and me, which suggested they had a source of airline information. With knowledge of our flight, they may have briefed a third party to look out for us at the airport and then to follow us. This would explain how they had quickly located our accommodation.

It seemed they had contacts in London, as they had been visited twice during the night, at around 11.30 pm and just after midnight.

After these brief meetings they had escorted their visitors out. One had been followed by our team, both on foot and on the tube. The fellow had gone back to a room in a high-rise social housing block which was used to accommodate new immigrants.

Rupert said that Florence's mobile phone had been used extensively for international calls, and for a number of local calls too.

"How on earth do you know that?" I asked.

"We have friends in the telecommunications world," replied Rupert. "It's not difficult for them to access this information. We also found out that they're using their own names. We expected this, as they would have needed to show identification and paid deposits etc. to book in. Easy stuff.

"As a precaution," he continued, "we fitted a GPS transmitter to the EO van. We also put a miniature Wi-Fi, IP camera into the hallway of their hotel." He brought up an image on his phone. It showed the hotel corridor; someone was walking along it. I told him It wasn't one of them.

"No," Rupert replied. "We know what they look like now. The camera is being constantly monitored by another colleague of ours, Whim." He took a breath before continuing, "He's also my partner – a most reliable chap, and the personification of vigilance."

"I'm sure Whim will be of great help," I replied. "We are most privileged and grateful to have all this wonderful support."

"Not at all," said Rupert with a nod, clearly pleased that this latter part of our interchange had gone well.

Penelope had been listening quietly. "We anticipate, Paul dear," she said, "that you will get a telephone call soon. We would like you to answer it when it rings. It will likely be from Florence, with instructions for you. They'll probably ask you to taxi to them. If not, we'll modify our plans accordingly. We'll get you ready to go. Our plan is to fully comply with the EO instructions. This seems the best way to secure Florence's wellbeing."

I gave my consent with a small nod.

"The courier depot is in North London," she continued. "If needs be, we can either second someone from our team to the courier company, or actually uplift the courier altogether – although we would be getting into murky territory by doing that. You'll have to stay with one of them while Florence goes in with the other to collect the parcel. Then Florence and whichever of them it is, would join the other EO and you."

"Yes, that seems the likely scenario," I said.

"After they have the note," Penelope went on, "they may release you. You must give them the cash that you'll take with you, too. They'll know there's a chance you and Florence might go to the police; consequently they may hold you both until they leave the country."

"Yes," I agreed.

"We haven't uncovered any of their travel plans, but they may have booked under false names," she continued.

"Paul," interjected Rupert, "we will prioritise your safety and Florence's. We'll be close at hand throughout the entire undertaking. Indeed, for all scenarios we have a sound plan. Should we need to physically intervene at any stage, then we can do that. We'll avoid violence or any sort of fracas, but we'll be prepared for it too."

"Indeed. No violence please," I said.

Sedgey continued, "There will be others of our greater team involved, but you need not know about them, and may not see them. These are more of our competent friends. Paul, this operation is easy meat for us, and you mustn't worry about things. Tonight, once everything's sorted out, I expect we'll all be sitting down to a slap-up dinner, Florence included."

"Your team is amazing," I replied. "I'm truly in awe. I'll do just as you instruct. It's unbelievable that you have done so much and in no time at all. I will play my part willingly. I'm not afraid for my old skin – I'm well in credit with regards to my allocation of life. I worry greatly for Florence, though. She's already been brutally beaten by Boona. And being a drug-infused psychopath, she'd think nothing of killing Florence. Take care, please, for Florence's sake."

Sedgey nodded.

"I'm happy to accept the consequences, if you think it best to go to the actual police," I continued. "I know you're taking every precaution, but I hate the thought of anyone being hurt." I looked them both in the eye. "I thank and salute you all." I put my hands together in the namaste and bowed my head to them.

Soon I was dressed, and we were 'rolling' not much later. I had received the anticipated phone call, feeling a sinister chill when I heard Boona's cold, clearly enunciated tones. She instructed me that a taxi would arrive within fifteen minutes, and that it would take me to a place where I would be picked up by them. She concluded, "I will kill the bitch if you try anything on."

Sedgey told me to do just as they asked. The team would be there with me, all the way, although I wouldn't see them.

Penelope watched at the window for the taxi as I sat quietly waiting. Before long she said, "Your taxi is here, Paul dear. Take your time now, behave like an old man. I will help you into it. The taxi's genuine, so when I lean in to fasten your seat belt, I will drop a GPS tracker into the magazine pocket. Just a little insurance, as we will be following the taxi. Now, off we go."

A black London taxi sat tick-ticking quietly in the driveway.

"Need a hand, Gov?" asked the driver.

"I'll help him in, thank you," answered Penelope with a smile.

I could have managed very well on my own, but I let Penelope take my arm and ease me into the seat. As she reached across for the seat belt, she pushed a small cloth bag deep into the magazine pocket in the back of the driver's seat.

"Do have a good day, Mr Moody," she said, and with a small pat on my hand, moved back out of the cab.

"All good to go, Gov?" asked the cabbie. I answered in the affirmative, and we moved off down the street.

We travelled through suburban streets for some time, perhaps fifteen minutes, before stopping at a loading zone in a large shopping complex. I didn't know where I was.

"Here we go, Gov – all prepaid. I'll hop around and help you out," said the cabbie.

"I can manage, thanks – need the exercise anyway," I answered. Then I shuffled across the seat and pulled myself up and out of the taxi. A semi-suppressed grunt of exertion later, and without too much trouble, I was on the footpath. I gave the driver a two-pound coin. We exchanged smiles; he waited until I'd moved back away from the taxi, and with a small wave, sedately moved off.

The shopping centre was busy. Adjacent to the entrance were several outdoor bench seats. It was pleasant outside, so I walked to the nearest of these and sat down. Soon, my phone rang. It was Boona. Her cold, clipped, tones instructed me to, "Go into the mall for fifty metres and you will see another, smaller entranceway. Go down that and wait outside. Understand?"

"Yes," I answered.

Boona ended the call. I started out, first moving through the mall with its attractive hustle and bustle (but loud, unattractive music), and then down the entranceway and out onto the street.

I stood back from the road, panting a little. So far so good. I felt calm enough, although the situation seemed surreal.

Life bustled around me.

I was an actor in a film.

After a short time, a small green car pulled up and the passenger door was pushed open. I moved to the car, stooped, and looked inside. It was neither Boona nor Dhama.

"Have you come to collect Paul Moody?" I asked of the driver, who remained seated and staring directly ahead. Without turning he gave a grunt and a nod. I got into the car; this was awkward to do, as it was small and low to the ground. I half fell the final way into the seat.

I shut the door behind me and the vehicle moved off. Both the car and the driver were silent. Perhaps it was one of these new electric cars, I thought.

We moved through the streets, in and out of the busy traffic, and soon joined a major road. Then we were on a motorway and moving quickly. Unexpectedly the driver passed me a plastic bottle of water. I realised I was thirsty, and drank deeply.

Time passed; we had been travelling now for perhaps thirty minutes.

The driver held out his hand. "Give phone," he instructed in a thick accent. I did as he asked, and he put it into his jacket pocket.

We exited the motorway into a service station, and the driver parked in a distant part of the mostly empty car park. He got out and moved off a short distance, then made a call on his phone. After a short conversation he returned to the car and handed his phone to me.

"Paul – is it you?" Florence's clear, anxious voice asked.

"Yes, my dear, it is me. I'm alright, but I have no idea where I am. Are *you* alright? You must do exactly as they ask, Florence. I expect they want to go and get their note and will take you to the depot to sign for it."

"Yes, Paul. That is what they want, and they are saying that if we do anything to raise alarm, they will hurt us. You must do what they want. OK? They tell me that if they are getting what they want, they will let both of us go tomorrow morning. They are here now. I need to go and do as they are wanting. Paul, I think we should be OK. Fine. But I worry about you."

"I am doing well, my dear. You just go and do whatever they want, we'll see each other soon."

The phone went dead. My driver held out his hand and I returned it to him.

We set off again, and drove into central London. The driver parked in a disabled car space, first putting a disabled sticker on the windscreen.

Then we walked a short distance to a ferry terminal near The Tower of London. The driver bought two tickets for a Thames River cruise, and before long we were on the ferry, travelling quickly downstream.

We're killing time while they go and pick up the courier package, I thought.

After a while the ferry turned around in a wide arc and we headed back upstream, going some way beyond our starting point. The ferry turned yet again and we headed back to the base.

The trip had taken about an hour. Headphones were provided and a commentary was available, but I didn't put them on, or take in the sights.

I was blank.

As we walked back to the car my host's phone rang. From the ensuing conversation I deduced that all had gone well, and assumed that we would now join the others. By gesture I was told to get into the car.

We drove again through the busy streets. Soon, much to my surprise, I recognised where we were – back in Kew, near the B&B.

The car stopped. The driver handed me my phone then told me to go.

"Go?" I mimicked, incredulously.

I was mystified as to their use of me. The driver turned away and adopted his forward-staring pose. I opened the door and, with some difficulty, pulled myself up and out of the car.

The car silently glided off, and I rather unsteadily made my way the short distance back to the accommodation. As I reached the front door it opened, and there stood Penelope.

"Paul, dear, there you are. Come in and sit down – you look all in. Before we speak you must have some tea." She took my arm and guided me in.

"I must say I'm fagged," I replied. "Heaven only knows where I've been, but part of the journey was a sightseeing trip on the Thames."

Penelope eased me into a comfortable chair in the sitting room. "Yes, we know what you've been up to, poor dear," she said. "The team have had you in their sights all the way. You were only back-up security. And they have got what they wanted. Just let me get your tea and I'll tell you all about developments."

"Is Florence alright?" I asked. "I'm very worried for her."

"Yes, she's fine, as best we can tell. We guess the EO will have her released after they leave the country. It's better for them if no harm comes to Florence at present. Back in a tick with the tea."

I felt revived after my tea and fruit cake. Penelope helped me back to my bedroom, and I lay on top of my bed, shoes off, my head propped up by pillows. I had a much-needed rest.

The nerve centre – the sitting room next door – was abuzz with activity. I could distinguish the vocal tones of each of the four participants: Sedgey's deliberate phrasing and clear, cultured voice; Moose's excessive volume and frequent guffawing, and the softer, mellifluous and charming tones of Rupert and Penelope. The actual conversations I couldn't hear, but they seemed mainly to be making or taking telephone calls.

The sounds receded, becoming more distant. The rigours of the morning embraced me, and I was gently but firmly drawn into sleep.

Dreams came quickly: I was in the back yard of the property my first wife and I had purchased not long after we were married, all those years ago. The back yard was unformed, as was usual on a new property back then, and thanks to the incessant rain, it had turned mostly to mud. I was trying to dig this mud with a large shovel, which had become caked with yellow, sticky clay.

My wife stood on the back steps of the house. She wore a long cotton summer frock, pale blue with a white floral print. She looked immaculate, as usual. I was covered in mud and exasperated.

My wife was admonishing me for my lack of progress and general incompetence as a handyman. According to her, I should have been further on with the excavation of her much-desired meditation pit. Such a feature was popular at that time. By now I should have been laying the tiles around the pit's stepped terraces. These beautiful, iridescent, deep-blue tiles lay stacked nearby in neat piles, and as I sweated and panted, I registered the contrast of the tiles with the muddy, shallow, scrape of a home I was preparing for them.

My wife shook her head and retreated into the house, away from the pain of my ineptitude.

"I can do this," I'd said, when my wife had, at the outset of the project, insisted on bringing in expensive experts. Now, as I struggled, I felt sick, stuck in the no-mans-land between giving up and carrying on.

A few minutes later, my friend Albie Stocks put his head around the corner of the house.

"Looks like you need a hand, old bud?" he said with a smile.

Relief flooded over me; I suppressed my delight, but with a shrug and a nod, accepted his offer.

Alfie took over, and I was appointed Doer of Small Tasks – as a means of keeping me from impeding the real progress.

My wife was back again, standing on the top step. Now she was smiling – mainly at Albie, who, with his muscles and big grin, had managed in no time at all to neatly cut each of the required steps in the clay soil, and had now commenced laying out a smooth, even coating of sand on each terraced surface, in preparation for the laying of the tiles.

More sand would be needed for this, I realised, and so I quickly piled the wheelbarrow high with sand from the nearby pile. I lifted the handles of the barrow and set off with the load. The barrow was very heavy. I began to push; it wobbled, but it was reluctant to move forward – the damn thing seemed to have a mind of its own. It shifted a little, but then violently lurched to one side. I pushed harder and put my weight on one handle to right it. It would not be levelled, and it abruptly overturned. I fell with it. The sand spilled out onto the mud and all over Albie's good work.

My wife's mouth contorted with distain, muttering words I couldn't hear.

My past stress and anguish, it would seem, were an analogue of my present hopelessness.

19

I was awake, and Penelope was back.

"Paul, I'm so sorry to disturb you. You must be worn out, poor soul. Unfortunately we have a small problem, and we may need your help. Did I give you a shock? Take a minute for yourself, my dear, then I'll come back for you."

There was a glass of water on my bedside table and I sipped from it while I took a minute to compose myself.

"Stupid old fool," I said out aloud, still affected by my dream.

Penelope returned, and we went through to the sitting room.

"Ah, Paul!" said Sedgy. "The EO are on the move. Moreover, there has been a call to your mobile phone, and we expect they'll try you again soon. We thought it best that you answer it when it rings. We know they're in two vehicles and are heading north on the motorway, possibly en route to another city with an international airport. Manchester, probably. They have both their van and the blue car they used to transport you in earlier on. We have checked out their erstwhile digs and no one remains there. Florence is with them, which may not be so good."

I could sense things weren't going as hoped.

Rupert continued, "We'd hoped they would clear out quickly from one of the London airports, and leave Florence behind. Now, given our concern for Florence and our bewilderment at their actions, whilst it's not appropriate to involve the police, we're considering some interventionist action to free Florence. We'll get cracking soon and will follow them so that we're close at hand to intervene, should we need to. We must keep Florence safe. The EO may intend keeping her as a hostage until just before they leave, or they may be thinking of taking her with them. Their present actions seem illogical."

"We must try and substitute me for Florence," I interjected. "I'm old and well past my useful time. I will ask them to swap us when they call."

"No. I think not," replied Sedgey. "They won't want you. You have no value to them; you would be more conspicuous and more trouble to transport. What we want is for you to pass on a message when they call you. You must tell them that you have private detectives helping you, and that these detectives have them under close surveillance. You'll be able to give them their exact location to verify this. Then you'll tell them they must release Florence, or we'll go to the police forthwith."

I nodded, but felt sick that the situation was running out of control.

Sedgey carried on, "They may threaten to hurt Florence. Tell them they have just one hour to think things over, then you'll phone them back to confirm the arrangements for Florence's release. By that time we'll have caught up to them. Their convoy has left the highway and is moving quite slowly through minor roads in the countryside. Lord knows why! We have an advance party very near to them. The rest of us will catch up with them quickly."

Before long my phone rang. It was Boona.

"Listen. To. Me. You old arsehole," she began. "The bitch is dead meat unless you do exactly what I tell you. We are out of here, and she is coming with us. You will say nothing to anyone. HEAR ME, you old prick. AND, you will transfer the rest of our money to a bank account that I will text to you. The bitch will be left behind at a stopover between our flights and will be looked after there until we have received the money from you. Then, maybe, she will get her passport back and we will let her go. Our stopover place is not a very nice one, especially when you get away from the tourist bits. We wouldn't like the silly bitch making it a lifelong stopover now, would we?" Boona sounded quite rational for a change, and seemed to be enjoying imparting her menacing message.

I was choked, and, more than ever, filled with hatred for her. "Boona …" I began, "we know where you are." The details were in front of me on a sheet of paper, and I was able to describe exactly where they were.

"What's more," I continued, in my surprisingly strong voice, "we have an army of private detectives monitoring your every move, and we know your travel plans. We were able to access this help using your money. Thank you for that! Moreover, the police and the airport authorities can be notified in an instant and, given that the authorities back in New Zealand are looking for you anyway, there will be no issue having you held here or anywhere, or with them coming to Florence's aid."

"DON'T TRY AND BLACKMAIL ME, SCUM!" shouted Boona.

I could see in my mind Boona's bulging bloodshot eyes and her red-veined, P-ravaged, face.

"DO WHAT I SAY, YOU STUPID OLD BASTARD, OR THE BITCH WON'T MAKE IT TO THE AIRPORT."

The phone disconnected.

"Bravo!" responded Sedgy. "Perfect. The EO are on the run and are well rattled. We must get going immediately, and intercept them. They'll be witless with panic after that exchange with you, knowing we're onto them, and that they can easily be exposed to the police."

Minutes later we were hurtling down the motorway in a high-powered six-seater SUV, well concealed within its darkened windows. Extreme as my concern was for Florence, I was excited. I hadn't taken my youth-promoting supplements for some days, but I felt strong, invigorated.

We would rescue Florence and all live happily ever after. I knew that now.

Several hours passed. We left the motorway and drove along country lanes to the south and east of Manchester. Sedgey spent much of his time on the phone, and advised us that the forward party had the EO in sight. They were travelling slowly and, for some reason, taking a circuitous route.

After some discussion with the rest of us, Sedgey asked the lead group to make sure that the EO knew they were being followed. His opinion was that, with this intimidation, they might dump Florence and make a run for the airport.

Further minutes passed. Then, with an edge of anxiety in his voice, Sedgey told us that the EO had driven in behind an abandoned cluster of old shops just beyond a rural village, and had stopped there.

“Not the best development, I think,” said Penelope. “Holing up suggests they prefer a confrontation to making a run for it. You know them, Paul, dear. Do you think it likely they would risk a fight and the likely exposure and capture that would ensue?”

I thought briefly. “They’re probably fully stoked on drugs and alcohol, and are probably sleep deprived as well. They’ll be functioning in an irrational haze, I should think. We must take extreme care; I feel Florence is in grave danger and we will be too if we confront them. I believe we should back off. It may be best just to let them go altogether, or when they get to the airport, try and snatch Florence. They’ll need to act with restraint at the airport.”

I began to feel ill with worry and stress, and quite panicky too. We clearly had little control of the developing situation. I tried to clear my head, but anxiety washed over me.

The others were talking amongst themselves. There was urgency in their voices, and though their words were clear I couldn’t concentrate enough to follow what they were saying.

We pulled over to the side of the road, in behind a white car, which apparently contained our forward team. Everyone got out of their vehicles and stood talking in an adjacent farm driveway.

“You stay there, Paul,” Penelope said as she got out. “I’ll brief you when I come back.”

Our group talked together for some minutes. Two were younger men I hadn’t seen before. The discussion seemed to centre around them.

After a few minutes our group returned to the SUV. They told me that the EO and Florence were in a vehicle parked under a large, dilapidated lean-to at the back of the row of old shops. Dhama had been making one telephone call after another and Boona was pacing about, smoking and swigging from a whisky bottle.

Our team felt that the EO were awaiting instructions, or taking advice, from a remote third party. It seemed unlikely they would stay where they were for much longer.

There was strained air of anticipation amongst us. Penelope told me the group wanted me to phone the EO on Florence's number, and to tell them that if they let Florence go, we would allow them to leave here, and indeed the country, without any sort of intervention.

"They won't trust us," I replied. "Boona, especially. She'll be agitated and irrational. I can talk to them, but I think I should say we'll give them the money. I have most of it here with me. Also, I think we should tell them we won't follow them, but that they must leave Florence at the airport, or we'll immediately contact the authorities both here and at home. And we shouldn't just say this – we should actually do it."

After more discussion we decided to give them the money as I had suggested, and that we should let them go and make it appear we had discontinued our surveillance.

I telephoned Florence's number. Boona answered. She screamed at me – it wasn't a conversation; it was a particularly unpleasant string of expletives. She intended smashing me and Florence to bits, she said, and would deal with my "poxy mates". She paused after this initial rant, and the fact that I was offering to give back the money may have penetrated her fog. I reemphasised this, saying slowly and clearly, "We will bring you the money shortly." I hung up.

I was shaken by Boona's wild aggression. She was indeed evil incarnate. I was frightened too; I couldn't imagine how poor, dear Florence was feeling. I knew in my heart that the best thing was to give them the money and let them go.

The concern from my colleagues had become palpable. I easily convinced them this was the only immediate course of action. The next-best option would have been to phone the police, although on this point there was unanimous disagreement from the rest of the team – each of whom held the police in rather low esteem. There was no time left for this course of action, anyway.

Our vehicles moved to within one hundred metres of the EO camp and I set off, teetering down the access driveway towards the shops. I held the supermarket bag of money out in front of me. The younger men on our team stood out in the open with rifles in their hands. The situation was cloaked in a dark and sinister veil. We all knew things were out of hand, but also that there was no going back.

Events had taken command of us.

I was to go close to them, put the money bag down on the ground and then tell them that, if they released Florence, we would withdraw and let them go, and wouldn't follow them or obstruct their escape in any way.

No one was in sight as I approached the EO's vehicles. I called out. No response. I decided to go on further. I moved forward and tentatively eased my way around the back of their van.

I was falling. I had been struck hard on the side of the head. I was on the ground.

A muffled gunshot rang out:

Boona was down too.

There must have been a member of our team somewhere on the adjacent roof with a clear view of us. Boona was lying across me.

Abruptly, her elbow crunched into my ribcage as she pushed herself off me and up onto her knees. She unsteadily got to her feet. I was lying on my side, and could see her clearly. Her jaw was clenched and her eyes bloodshot and staring. Behind her I could see Dhama and beside him, Florence.

Dhama gripped Florence by the arm. She was bleeding from her nose and forehead. She looked strong and defiant, and I gained strength from her. But I was hurt.

I couldn't hear.

Boona had got a gun from somewhere nearby. It was a handgun with a long barrel. *Boona and Dhama are off the planet*, I thought. *They are beyond reason.*

They moved back out of sight of the roof, taking Florence with them. Boona's gun had a silencer on it, and I saw the gun recoil in her hand as she discharged it in the direction of our group. I tried to raise myself up, but couldn't. Boona might have been crazed, but I saw her pick up the money bag. It looked as though they were going to their van. Hopefully they would make a run for it. If they did, surely our team would pull back and let them go.

Boona had been wounded somewhere under her left arm, but this didn't seem to affect her. There was a large, dark blood stain on her top, but perhaps the wound was superficial. Dhama had crawled to the side of the van and had reached up and opened the door. He got in and crouched down under the windscreen. The van started and he reversed it back further under the canopy. I moved my head so that I could see down the access lane. There were heads and rifle barrels above the bonnet of the white car.

Our team has welcomed this confrontation, I thought. How stupid I felt. Here we had the desperados at the end of their years of scummy criminality and depravation, and also the old professionals – the highly trained old professionals – not wanting to let go, welcoming the situation, probably willing for it to explode completely.

I was a silly old fool. I prayed that Florence would live to have some sort of future. For me, now – I didn't care.

I was falling. Not in a frightening way, but floating downward, spiralling through softness in a gentle light. I was comfortable – warm and supported. The past came back to me; it was floating too: an impressionist picture, in the way that the past becomes when you get very old.

A childhood of pastel shades enveloped me, along with comforting smells of old-fashioned gardens and home baking. Bare feet padded along dusty tracks in unfenced land that belonged to no one. Land seemingly left there for the children to claim by ancient right.

My spiralling descent drew to a stop. I was lying on lush grass beside a lively stream. The canopy of big trees leaned over me far above. Someone was with me. I didn't know who it was. I looked closely; my companion was an elderly man with a kindly face. He was speaking to me, the words silently floating from his mouth. It was an unknown text, but I could understand it.

He was gently admonishing me. And warning me. I turned away from him and looked up to the patches of light in the canopy above. It was restful here. I looked back; the man had gone. In his place was a small dog.

It was a miniature Border Collie. A beautiful little dog with intelligent eyes. He was looking at me. Was I his owner? He was expectant, awaiting instructions, wanting to embark on adventures.

Perhaps I was a boy again. My hands looked young. I felt like a boy.

A gentle wind blew up and with it rolled in a thin mist. I was standing now. The mist came only to the level of my waist; I waded slowly through it. The dog was beside me; I could not see him, but I could feel his soft body as he rubbed against my calves. I would call him Crispin and together we would find our way home. We were under the trees; the mist was fading away.

Someone was calling us: "Paul, Crispin, Paul, Crispin." We were being summoned but there was no urgency in the call. The voice was Florence's. I tried to answer her. My mouth was dry, my brain wouldn't focus. Florence had my hand. I could see her, yet my eyes wouldn't open.

Sometime towards the end of the big fight I had taken another blow to the head. Florence had been grazed in the neck by a bullet from a pistol and Boona had been hit by a second rifle shot.

Boona was dead.

Moose had received a minor gunshot wound to his abdomen. Our side prevailed and Dhama was captured.

I had been unconscious throughout all of this.

I was lying, head and shoulders propped up, in a hospital bed in a sunlit room in what seemed to be a bedroom in a private home. I later found out that it was a medical clinic that had been established in an old cottage on the air force base.

A cultured voice penetrated the slowly retreating fog. "We've had you a little sedated, old chap. Sorry about that."

"How many?" I said. I heard myself say this, but knew it wasn't what I wanted to say. What did I want to say? I drifted back into sleep.

Next time I woke more fully. I forced my eyes into focus. It seemed very bright, although the only light was softly dappled sunlight. Someone was sitting in a chair. I concentrated hard and focused: it was Florence. My heart lifted. I could see that she was smiling, albeit it was a rather concerned smile.

"My god," I groaned.

"Paul," Florence replied. "We are OK now. Both of us."

She got out of the chair and sat gently on the side of my bed. "You had big kick on your head by that bad one, Boona, and you haven't been too good for a few days, but you are a very strong one Paul, and you get better fast. I have been very worried."

She ruffled my hair gently and asked again if I was OK.

"I am not feeling any pain," I said. "Things are rather foggy, though, and suspect I will feel rather worse when whatever they have me on wears off."

As I came to properly, the questions rushed in. "Florence – who are these people? Penelope and her mates? Why are we not in a proper hospital? And look at you – all those bandages and your arm in a sling. What on earth has been going on?"

"I tell you more about this later," she said. "It mostly is that the Winston Churchill Village, and the other ones of that company, are in what they call a money launder thing; also involved in drug selling. All this seems connected with bad country governments. Terror stuff, maybe. This why is not a usual matter for the police. These things not good for the public and the news report. These people – our friends, our helpers – are sort of police too. When we check in the B&B they already know who we are, and what has happened to us – all of it, seems. Believe this, Paul?

Perplexed, I involuntarily leant forward from the pillows. "Surely not, Floral." I had reverted to her real name, as she had done with mine.

"Yes," continued Floral, "when we book that B&B, Penelope moved in first with her people. They were not who they told us, but really work for the government – apparently do. Yes, something like this. These people can be doing whatever is they like. Seems so, Paul. They now have told me everything, they say. They say sorry for using us. We tangle into a serious thing for sure. Much trouble – serious government matter. I not fully understanding all about it."

"Good Lord!" I exclaimed. "That scummy Boona was a threat to world governments! I simply cannot believe all this."

"Them, Boona and friends, only small fish, as you would say, Paul. Anyway, this is what Penelope tells me, she says Boona and the others they can lead to big matters, other people. This is what they tell me anyway. I have not been feeling too good myself, so have not been properly listening either. We will find out more soon. But they have been very good to me, anyway."

Floral paused and sipped from the glass of water on my bedside table, then pressed on with resolve. "They have taken away the last one of the EO – Dhama, who's now in prison, I think. This is the best I can describe these things. We are not in big trouble. Rupert is also telling me Penelope is the big boss and properly high up. Very amazed about that for sure! But they are saying we not in big trouble and they know nothing about the money, which we should not mention too, seeing as it not officially exists. Well! I cannot believe what happened. They shooting Boona dead at the fight, they says he was a very bad person much more so than we know, and that being dead pretty good outcome for everyone. Yes, pretty much seems to me that we agree on that one. I'm so happy you look better now, Paul. I have been very worried for you, my friend."

Over the following days, Floral and I remained at the cottage. We were both mending well, but were still in shock. I was comprehensively interviewed by a gentleman who, though in plain clothes, claimed to be a policeman and part of some sort of terrorist squad or the like. He looked more like a lawyer to me.

I told him absolutely everything, as truthfully as I could – the whole story, right from the beginning. As the words tumbled from my mouth, they seemed unreal, even to me. And, as unlikely as it all was, given the car chase and the gun fight, the policeman seemed to accept that the story was true. Moreover, he seemed to enjoy the tale, chuckling at various points.

Floral brought me our wonderful elixir-of-life supplements. She upped the dose somewhat, and consequently I was soon feeling much stronger. This unexpected healing progress left my unknowing, learned doctor astounded.

"Quite remarkable progress for an older gentleman," he said. "Mind you, everything about you is rather remarkable, old chap, I must say!"

After a long meeting with Penelope and her team, we were encouraged to get on with our lives but to stay within the bounds of Europe, so as to remain relatively safe and be contactable. Indeed, they furnished us with a shiny new passport each. Mine was in the name of Paul Cyrus McElhinney, and Floral's was in the name of Florence Doll Bantroosa. And although it wasn't official, we kept our money. It must have been too difficult for the authorities to rationalise, or perhaps the size of the sum hadn't been passed on to the hierarchy.

Sedgey advised us, in private and in hushed tones, that in regards these luscious funds, the less said the better, and I believe our helpers considered this an extension of their help, as they surely wouldn't have wanted to leave us stranded and destitute.

Now, as far as the world at large was concerned, our old identities no longer existed. Death notices for our previous selves were recorded in Britain, and were communicated to the authorities back home.

The time when we would go back out into the world was quickly approaching. But what should we do? We had plenty of money, and I could draw a British pension. Florence could work. Moreover, we both had access to governmental health care and to all the social services. That we should stay together as a team was a fabulous thought for me, and it was a comfort that Florence insisted this was what she wanted too.

The background bios we had been given to accompany our new names were sufficiently murky and vague, so that there would be no issues establishing a credible life wherever we wanted to go. Our 'Special Team' told us that if we needed to keep in contact with one or two people, this would be OK, providing we didn't reveal our location. We were instructed not to meet with anyone from the past. Phone calls could be OK. The prevailing wisdom was that although the scale of criminality we had become caught up in was high end, what had happened to us involved only the lowest level of the international criminal network, and that those at the higher levels – those who were of most interest to the authorities – would have no interest in us, and would be far more concerned with protecting those who were higher still – all, of course, in the interests of protecting their own sorry, criminal skins.

Florence became quite tearful on a few occasions, and I confess that at times, I felt rather frail and discombobulated too. This wasn't an effect of my injuries, although I had been properly knocked around; it was more from the PTSD effect. Shell shock, as it was known to my generation.

Our helpers offered to find us somewhere to go, ostensibly on holiday, so that we could regroup and take the time to decide what to do in a more permanent sense.

The place they found for us was a little stone fisherman's cottage on a beach just around the coast from Aberdeen in Scotland. To any people we might meet there, I was a wealthy old man convalescing from a significant medical treatment, which had gone particularly well, and I was now recovering in the clean Scottish air and enjoying the mild northern summer. As always, Floral was to be my nurse, my helper, and my faithful companion.

Looking back now, everything that immediately preceded this move is rather a haze: the relocation from the cottage hospital, and the journey up to Aberdeen. I recall that along the way there was a short flight, a limousine ride, and one or two taxi trips. It wasn't until a day or two later, when we were finally left on our own, that we had the clarity of thought to be able to take in our new surroundings. It was then that we realised we were in a picture-perfect tourist brochure.

Our stone cottage was very old, but it had been refurbished immaculately. It was by no means luxurious – in the five-star sense, anyway. Indeed, it was a little spartan, but it had everything we could need, and it was warm and tastefully decorated. Best of all, it sat right on the beachfront, and the view, and the immediate environment, were idyllic. We shopped in the town nearby and walked for miles along our lovely beach, convalescing, and in quiet, restorative contemplation.

The tender ships for the oil rigs came right in, close to our shoreline home as they approached the harbour, and although by no means the biggest vessels in the world, they seemed enormous to us and we felt that, had we reached out, we could have touched them. We had a sun umbrella and a couple of beach loungers at the property, and I spent many contented hours napping in the gentle warmth of the northern sun. At such times Florence usually preferred to keep busy in the cottage, preparing meals, studying English, and generally being busy in many little ways.

Penelope made an unexpected visit, and during a walk with her along our beach she told me of her loneliness after the passing of her husband some years before. She said she liked me and was keen to stay in contact. To be friends.

When I told Florence of this exchange she laughed, and with shining eyes teased me, making kissy movements with her mouth.

Whatever the future held for us, Florence and I were locked together in a bond which, whilst it wouldn't be romantic, would be yet a stronger one.

Brothers in arms, and true friends.

www.ingramcontent.com/pod-product-compliance
Lightning Source LLC
La Vergne TN
LVHW091319150826
845673LV00006B/1700

9780473670825